Tak

Taking It

a novel
Michael Cadnum

Viking

VIKING
Published by the Penguin Group
Penguin Books USA Inc., 375 Hudson Street, New York, New York 10014, U.S.A.
Penguin Books Ltd, 27 Wrights Lane, London W8 5TZ, England
Penguin Books Australia Ltd, Ringwood, Victoria, Australia
Penguin Books Canada Ltd, 10 Alcorn Avenue, Toronto, Ontario, Canada M4V 3B2
Penguin Books (N.Z.) Ltd, 182-190 Wairau Road, Auckland 10, New Zealand

Penguin Books Ltd, Registered Offices: Harmondsworth, Middlesex, England

First published in 1995 by Viking, a division of Penguin Books USA Inc.
Reprinted by arrangement with Penguin Books USA Inc.
10 9 8 7 6 5 4 3 2 1
Copyright © Michael Cadnum, 1995
All rights reserved

LIBRARY OF CONGRESS CATALOGING-IN-PUBLICATION DATA
Cadnum, Michael.
Taking it / by Michael Cadnum.   p.   cm.
Summary : Seventeen-year-old Anna Charles, who has turned shoplifting into
an art form and a way to vent frustration, feels her confidence crumbling
when she begins finding things she does not remember stealing.
ISBN 0-670-86130-8
[1. Shoplifting—Fiction.] I. Title.
PZ7.C11724Tak 1995 [Fic]—dc20   95-7881 CIP AC

Printed in USA
Set in Meridien

For Sherina

Quietly—
there are doves

··· 1 ···

The thing that made I. Magnin exciting was that the floorwalkers, the detectives who made sure you paid for everything you walked away with, were hard to spot.

In most department stores the security people carry paper shopping bags, except the bags are mostly empty. There is just a little weight at the bottom, a radio. You can tell if you know what to look for. Normal stores have security people dressed in such plain clothes you wonder how they can afford to do any shopping. But the point is, at I. Magnin you don't wonder. You don't see them.

In I. Magnin they have house detectives who look great, cuff links, tailored suits. Plus they have the usual kind, tourist-looking couples in rumpled clothes, badly shaven men with the earmark shopping bags. You don't know who to watch out for, and that makes it exciting.

I promised myself I was just looking. Look at all that perfume, I said to myself. I squirted some on my wrist. I smiled at the clerk. I smelled myself. Nice.

I was not going to do it. I had promised myself

months before. No more. I was finished. Besides, you get rusty at it. It gets too dangerous.

I wasn't even thinking about it.

I was going to meet Mother at Nordstrom's in about forty-five minutes to pick out clothes for her to wear on her trip to Banff with Adler, a slightly delayed honeymoon, and all I could think was how much time I had to kill. She had told me I could buy one of those skirts I had seen in the Bergdorf Goodman catalog, calico, one of those flowing, flowery things I used to like last year, which shows how far from each other my mother and I were.

What was I supposed to do, look at the pigeons? Because if BART had not been on time, and the train late or stuck under the Bay the way it usually is, then I wouldn't have been in that situation.

So I decided it wouldn't hurt. I wasn't kidding myself. It wasn't that cigarette smoker's stone lie: hey, just one, that's all. This was really just for old times' sake, just for fun.

Department stores have that wonderful smell, powder puff and floor wax and maybe a little chocolate, although sometimes it's hard to say where the candy aroma comes from. Some stores don't even sell chocolates, but the smell is there. And the smell of new things, clothes no one has ever taken to the dry cleaners.

Mom had just married Adler Harrison, the world's sweetest man. Mom didn't have the sense to know all you wore on a vacation in Alberta is jeans and walking shoes. Mom gets nervous, while I take after Dad. We get nervous, too, but we like it.

I asked for the ladies' room, saying "women's lounge," making it sound like I wanted to go lie down and sip a potion and watch the banks of the Nile drift by. I slipped in after making it look like I had trouble finding it, hurrying through cosmetics, toward women's shoes, letting a look of exasperation explain my wandering.

I washed the perfume off my hand as well as I could. I looked into the mirror, my green eyes looking back out at me showing no emotion, no excitement at all. Me, a step ahead of everybody else. I look older than I am, at the butt end of my junior year of high school. I look like someone well into college, Daddy's girl from USC, doing some pre-Paris shopping.

I'm not one of those people who give themselves away as soon as they start talking. I know how to sound as smart as I look. The thing to do is don't change your expression, and look at everything like you saw a better one last week in London.

I used to dress all-natural, high-fashion farm girl. Stu said he liked that, but I think it was partly because a full skirt gets hiked up easier than black leather, like I used to wear back in the first months of my sophomore year. Today I was all-silk, navy blue blouse and skirt. Tasteful, a psychology major, maybe, but thinking about law school.

Some thrill. I made a deal with myself last time, but that was because I had to. I promised myself I would stop. It had gotten so bad the Emporium had someone meet me at the door every time I ran in to buy pantyhose. They never called the cops. I never gave them a chance for that, and besides, Dad would skin them alive.

I decided to make it easy on myself by picking out one of the big silk scarves, a teardrop pattern with what I took to be a hand-knotted fringe. I fell in love with a cabled cashmere sweater, and made a show of myself holding up the navy and then the green, the tissue paper falling out of each.

I held up the sweaters, turning from side to side, shaking my head. Mirrors fascinate me, the way the image stands in a world much smaller than the one we inhabit. We think: There I am.

I made a show of giving up on the sweaters, watching the shoppers and the clerks in the three-way mirror. Nobody was watching.

$$\cdots 2 \cdots$$

People have no idea how much you can get away with. They never even try, like people living beside a lake they never even go wading in, much less swimming.

Stores keep an eye on jewelry. They put it out on that little velvet tray, letting it spill into the light so you can admire the quality, or recognize the lack of it. But jewelry is just the right size if you want to have some fun, and I had an eighteen-karat Venetian bracelet in my hand, my fingers hooked so the overpriced halo hung there, catching the eye of the clerk in charge.

"I want to see the earrings," I said, pointing to the ones with rocks the size of horses' teeth.

There was an instant of pleasure. I knew. They had me. One of these people had looked in my direction once too often, passed by once again just a little too slowly. The clerk looked over my shoulder, a thin woman with the makeup on one eye just a little more hastily applied than on the other, making her right eye look slightly smaller.

"Not today," I said. "I'm sorry."

"That's quite all right," she said, smiling, good at it, in on what was happening.

Now the main effort would be to get me out of the store, out on the sidewalk, out in the sunshine across the street from Union Square, where the script would be very predictable.

The man in the navy pinstripe or the man in the white jogging shoes would open a door for me. And then the difficult part for them would be to cause the offending article, the stolen item, to tumble out of my person without seeming to touch me. They do it all the time, and what a pickpocket does routinely is so much more challenging.

I circled, stalling. I trailed my fingers among neckties, fingering men's undies, big silk ones with a Hawaiian motif, nothing like what Stu would wear, a little outrageous for this store. I admired the way perfume comes in so many shapes. No, I said with a smile, I already sampled some.

I was waiting, wondering how many security personnel would be in on the setup, and they were good. There was only one I was sure of, the man in the blue blazer. These people were all directed by someone sitting at a TV screen, and they were doing the job the way it ought to be done.

I pushed against the door, feigned mild surprise at the assistance shown me by someone apparently on his way in. What a disappointment—it was one of the scuzzy detectives, white Levi's and a button-collar shirt with the collar unbuttoned. He was a big man. Maybe they expected trouble, a teenager who was half banshee, all fingernails and maybe even a weapon, a nail file Super Glued to a stick.

The man was sucking a breath mint, and stopped sucking only for a moment, when he put a finger up my sleeve, and tugged.

You could tell just before he did it that he knew he was making a mistake. His finger crooked just a little, and had the look of a finger about to push the wrong button, or, in this case, reach in and find nothing. He gave it a good try. His finger pinched and tugged, felt in a little farther, and tugged again, but all he found was the sleeve of my navy blue silk blouse.

I fell back, like a person pushed hard. This was an exaggeration, pretty good acting. Then I bore down on the mint sucker, and it would have been technically legal if I had done something in self-defense, a push of my own, a woman fighting back against open animal behavior. I took a course after school, and I know what to do, where the outline of the body was decorated with red arrows: Kick here.

We were surrounded by people in suits, and you could tell what they were thinking. They were thinking: Don't touch her. Don't lay a hand on this little woman with the blouse that suddenly slipped down off one shoulder, bra strap and wide-eyed innocence, and shock, and tears.

They were thinking, whatever else we did we didn't touch her. Did we?

The manager was a woman with fine bones and high cheeks, someone who didn't have to pretend to be bored.

"We get wealthy women in here, well-known, good people. You might be surprised. They try to leave with cosmetics, a pair of gloves. Nothing of any particular value. They want to be caught, I think."

I smiled, waiting. I was a little irritated because she was not irritated, or embarrassed. It's no fun if you don't watch them squirm when they realize who I am.

She continued, "It wasn't the scarf. It wasn't the bracelet. It was the bit with the sweaters."

Bracelet, I thought. Who would want one of those? "My Dad won't like this," I said.

"I know," she said thoughtfully.

"You have to train your people to be more careful."

There was a knock, and the navy and the green sweaters were both brought in by the scuzzy detective. He even gave me a nod, but he didn't leave.

The manager unfolded the green sweater and shook out what looked like the teardrop-pattern scarf. "You like to tease, don't you?"

She was indulging herself now. She had that mix of refinement and experience that allowed her to say whatever she wanted. I have an aunt like that, my mother's older sister. My aunt wouldn't marry anyone like Adler, who thought a trip to Lake Louise was great fun.

The manager was smiling, being nice about it. Besides, she recognized a change in me. I was suddenly not so self-assured.

I was unable to say anything, unable to so much as twitch.

This was not the teardrop scarf. This was another scarf entirely, one I had never touched.

··· 3 ···

"I've never seen that scarf before," I said. My voice came out sounding really bad, crinkly and childlike, a nine-year-old about to cry.

She waved a finger, dismissing this remark.

But it was true. It was going to be wonderful, perfectly great, I raged silently at myself, if after years of toying with this little sport of mine I got into real trouble over something I had never even put a pinky on. This was a scarf with little yellow triangles, a nice scarf, but not the one I had picked up.

The manager considered the scarf in her hands, and my new driver's license, which she had lined up so that the card fit the corner of her desk exactly. Anna Teresa Charles, my license read, with my weight now inaccurate by two pounds and my hair too blonde. I use a rinse to keep it dark.

I must be losing something, I thought. It happens. Or, even more likely—I'm deliberately screwing up.

They'd love nailing me, a daughter of one of the Big Names in town, always getting his photo in the *Chronicle* over a few column inches describing an out-of-court settlement. None of the stores had ever got where they could hurt me. I suddenly hated this woman with her lip-colored lipstick, and her tasteful mascara, done so right you wouldn't think she was wearing any.

I was seventeen years old. It was time to give up stupid childish things. I never really committed a crime. I never even came close. But what if I made a Freudian goof, tucked something in a pocket when even I wasn't looking?

I was sweating and cold. There was a sour taste in my mouth.

"You can understand why we have to be careful," she said. She was not acting like any of the other managers, like she had me, and I knew she didn't.

I said, "Your security man put his hand on me."

"We have it on video," she said.

Like that proved something in their favor, not mine. "I didn't do anything."

She was fingering her way through a Rolodex. She found what she wanted.

"You can't keep me here," I said.

What she said next made me shut up. She wasn't talking to me, she was talking into the phone. She was identifying herself, giving her name, Jane Murray, speaking in one of those Genius Android voices that tell you the time.

"I'm fine, Hal," she said, calm and looking at me with an expression almost kind, but not quite. "But I think I can do you a favor." She listened, and laughed, not loud—kind, thoughtful, regretful. If my Dad wasn't with one of his personal therapists, he would be clear-headed enough to know what was coming.

How did she know him?

I could hear his voice, reduced to a fly-size buzz. It was him, no question. "Yes, very personal," she said, sounding a little sexy, the way my dad got every woman to sound, sooner or later.

Every time I feel like this I think if I close my eyes I can imagine what it's like to be a thousand miles away, in the middle of a desert. I can picture it, cactus, sand, ants. Or a thousand miles up, cold, ocean down there, big clouds, my skin ice.

"Your daughter is here," she was saying into the phone. "Right here in my office. I think we need to talk."

··· 4 ···

My brother says that we don't know anything about anything. He said the Greeks knew how to think. He says all we are doing is filling out the questionnaires they left around, *Examine Your Life and Make It Worth Living*, those *Twenty Questions That Will Improve Your Sex Life* quizzes you see in magazines.

I hurried past shops, and didn't bother watching my reflection in the windows I passed. Don't think, I told myself. Just shut up and walk.

The Bay Area Rapid Transit stations are sometimes surrounded by people who look like trouble, people with nothing to do but look at you hard and ask for money. But when you take the escalator down into the subway station, you're in a different world. The light is bright, and steel machines take your dollar bills when you feed them into a slot and then give you a ticket.

Sometimes one of the dollars is too wrinkled, and the machine won't swallow it. Then you have to stand there trying to straighten out the wrinkled piece of money. People line up behind you, but they tend to act patient and a little bored because this happens to everyone.

I took BART back across under the Bay, heading east and not thinking, reading a *Chronicle* I found on the floor, the horoscope saying my romantic life was on hold. I looked for an article by Adler, one of his

11

columns on how to live a better life, but I couldn't find anything but want ads and a weather map.

Sometimes it's hard to breathe as the train roars through the tunnel under the Bay. You might not see sunlight again.

I got out of the BART station, the machine spitting out my ticket with twenty cents left. I gave the ticket to a man with a cat tied to a long piece of red yarn.

I got into the Mustang, which I should have taken across the Bay, except that I was trying to conserve gasoline the way we are supposed to, and the last time I tried driving in the City, I scraped the chrome off the right front bumper getting out of a parking place in a hurry.

Dad gave me the car because of my grades, a '67 automatic transmission with a new paint job and new vinyl interior, but the car had an old, tired smell, and I had already gotten a ticket for going eighty through the Caldecott Tunnel, although that was not my fault. Stu was with me that night, pissing me off talking about how I should get more exercise, take up jogging.

I had to stand there in the BART parking lot, yanking at the door. It wouldn't open. I was tugging at the car so hard the chassis was rocking. My feeling was that the car was in a collision at an earlier point in its history, and that it never entirely recovered.

I finally got inside, and then I had to wait for the interior of the car to cool. The steering wheel was too hot, and I don't have one of those cardboard windshield screens. I tried to crank down one of the windows and it would lower only about one-fifth of the way.

———

"You look strange," said Maureen.

I wanted to tell Maureen what had happened, but one look at her told me she had her own problems, as usual. "There's nothing wrong with me," I said. I stood peeking through the living room curtains of her house. My own house was across the street.

"You look . . ." Her voice faded. "Anxious."

I wanted to tell her all about the manager, how she and my father had a nice long talk while I was asked to go sit in a room full of computers, one thin old woman there looking at me like she was typing up a police report. She was one of those scary-looking old women, all string and dyed hair, and half-lens glasses, typing two hundred words a minute into a computer.

"You're the one who looks like a disaster area," I said.

"I feel like I've been kicked in the gut," said Maureen.

We were both afraid to talk to our fathers that night. What I had done was much worse, but Maureen isn't used to trouble. Maureen's mother was always gone, away on business. Her family left notes for each other, Post-Its with smiling faces all over the fridge.

"You're proud of how much you suffer," I said. Some friends play tennis. Maureen and I argue.

"You have no basic appreciation for what I'm going through," she said. Maureen was lying on the sofa in the front room, wearing gym shorts and a LOVE ANI-MALS DON'T EAT THEM T-shirt. She moved her head around on the pillow, looking for a position that was comfortable. She gave up and threw the pillow onto the floor.

She had dropped one of her father's favorite vases, a black clay flower container from Mexico. I had helped her sweep the black bits of it into a dustpan and suck up the rest of it with a portable Eureka Maureen kept in her room.

Maureen's family has cute art from all over. A yellow giraffe was one of my favorites, and a little blue frog on the fireplace always caught my eye. You could make a National Geographic special about these shelves, "Handmade Treasures from the Jungle." The carpet was worn from the kitchen to the dining room, and the TV had an old-fashioned remote, one you had to push hard to change channels, but it was plain where all the money went.

Maureen was talking, but I wasn't really listening. I was thinking that maybe someday I'd have a house like this, pretty art, visitors dropping by to see how interesting I was, cheerful notes reminding people to put out the recycling.

"On a day like this I even wish it wasn't summer," said Maureen. "I'd rather be in school."

"Even in Mr. Hewlett's class?" I asked.

Maureen couldn't help laughing, shaking her head. Mr. Hewlett was an English teacher whose favorite phrase was "Let's take a second and review." He taught right out of the *Words and Usage* book and never skipped a page. He was so boring you were sure there was something wrong with him, something medical, genetic.

Maureen said, "Remember that time you told him he could go home if he wasn't feeling well?"

Maureen and I always sat together when we shared a class. She doodled a lot when she was bored, filling her notes with stars and planets.

We were quiet for a moment, enjoying each other's company. Half the time I couldn't stand Maureen, but the rest of the time she was like a force of nature, terrible weather that could turn sunny and then, after a while, turn back again.

"The pain I feel," said Maureen, "is real."

"You agonize more than anyone who ever lived," I said. I meant it as a kind of compliment. "Seventeen years of torture."

"I saw a woman on television who looks the way you'll look in a couple of years," said Maureen.

"Beautiful woman, right?" I wandered away from her. There was a smell of yeast in the kitchen, and dough drowsed under the plastic dome of a bread machine. There was a bunch of purple onions, and a row of small-to-machete knives on the wall. Maureen was the only person I knew who made yogurt, and her father sometimes made hand-cranked ice cream.

Back in the living room, Maureen was waiting for me, and started in again. "She had these big pores, you could see even on the TV screen. Too much makeup, the skin not being able to breathe."

And then I remembered. I felt sick.

I had forgotten my mother. She was waiting for me at Nordstrom's, all the way across the Bay. I was two hours late.

Three hours late by now.

And nobody makes my mother wait.

... 5 ...

"Also, she was really gaunt and her hair was all over the place." It took me a moment to follow what Maureen was talking about, some person on TV. I was standing there looking at a ceramic poison-arrow frog and realizing that I was losing my mind.

I could call Nordstrom's, I thought. I could have my mother paged. I could make up a story, a flat on the Nimitz Freeway, the AAA tow truck stuck in traffic. I could tell her I got sick, stomach flu. But my mother would have gone home by now, or over to Gump's to buy another gold fountain pen to add to Adler's collection.

I don't believe in astrology, but sometimes I can feel what is happening out in space, how it pulls on my insides one way and another, like tides. By now my mother was thinking of ways to kill me.

It would be like the old days, real fury. It must be like this when you realize you're getting Alzheimer's disease. Little things go wrong. Or even worse, it must be like this when you start to go insane.

"Do you want to know how the vase got broken?" Maureen asked.

It was a relief to be able to keep talking. "You said you dropped it."

I went over to a mirror on the wall, the glass framed with carved purple bananas.

"That's not what I said," Maureen replied.

Nobody could tell by looking at me what I was feeling. I gave Maureen one of my best expressions, a sophisticated woman faced with someone less fortunate than herself. Inside I was shriveling. "Tell your dad that I picked it up and threw it at you."

"I'm not so afraid he'll be angry," said Maureen. "It's more like—I can't bear to see the look in his eyes."

I wanted a cigarette, but Maureen wouldn't let me smoke in her house. It gave her asthma. Her father was a professor at Cal at the school of optometry, and her mother helped write the bar exams used by each state. She was always calling from distant hotel rooms, lecturing in Milwaukee or Tucson. None of them smoked, but they left big red and purple ashtrays all over, Aztec-style pottery you could stub out your Marlboro in.

Maureen lifted her head again. She was looking right at me, and she had no idea how I felt. "I get these cramps when I'm upset," she said. Maureen and I had been in the same ballet class about a hundred years ago.

Maureen is pretty but she doesn't care about her looks, lets her eyebrows grow in so they meet, making her look serious all the time, like some kind of thinking animal. And it makes her look pretty anyway, the way a raccoon is pretty.

"I'll tell you what really happened," Maureen was saying.

She paused so I could ask, but I had trouble reading my lines for a second.

"Lincoln did it." She said this like it was a major revelation. She added, "I'm not supposed to let Lincoln into the house."

I had to feel compassion for Maureen. She didn't think about things—she experienced them. If she was depressed, she got sick. If she laughed too much, she peed.

"Poor Lincoln," I said. "Chained up in the backyard all the time." I heard my own voice, and reassured myself. I couldn't be a total mess if I could make conversation.

"Are you sure you're all right?" asked Maureen.

I peeked out the living room window. "The pool man's here," I said. "I can see his truck."

"I bet he has a tattoo, somewhere where you can't see it," said Maureen.

"He does not," I said, laughing. Maureen and I had both agreed we loathed tattoos on men.

"But you don't know for sure," she said.

I wanted to tell her that I didn't know anything for sure.

As always, Lincoln was excited to see me, and barked, and yelped, the animal trying to make words but not able to, having a snout and not a mouth. He was a big, dark dog on a frayed leather leash. A choke collar looped around his neck, a glittering chain.

Lincoln licked my hands, making them all hot and sticky. Lincoln's leash had worn all the grass from that part of the garden, and he bounded around on the bare dirt.

Maureen's family had chosen Lincoln at the animal shelter. He was nervous around strangers and had a strong dislike—even a fear—of anyone in uniform. He was perhaps the only dog in the world to actually flee into a distant room when the mailman approached.

I was fond of Lincoln, but I'm not crazy about dog spit. I let myself out through the side gate and washed my fingers off on a faucet beside the Boston ferns.

The blue pool truck was parked right behind the Mustang. I tried to like the white, sporty thing, but it was not a car I would have chosen myself. It was hard to park, and I felt a little guilty about wanting a car that didn't use so much gas.

I opened the front door and called out, asking if anyone was home. Maybe my mother was here, I thought. She had taken the day off so we could spend some time together. She might be pacing up and down, chewing her fingernails.

Maybe Dad had come home early, thinking that he had to talk to me, find out what was wrong with me, make an appointment for me to talk to someone in family counseling. I couldn't face him, not the way I felt now.

There was no one there. I listened hard and there was only the sound of the pool man whistling a tune to himself.

My fingers were cold, the way they get if I smoke too much. I took out the hoops and went to put in the gold posts. I don't like to swim wearing big earrings— they tend to drag in the water. I had trouble finding the holes in both lobes.

...6...

The pool man comes twice a week. He wears those shirts you buy that already look old, thick cotton with three buttons you leave undone if you want to show off your tan.

The pool man was crouching beside the water, one of those men with blond hair and muscles. He was losing his hair a little. Some men get bald and they look bony and too big for everything, like they're running out of hair because there is so much skin to cover.

But this guy always looked like a tennis instructor, one of those guys with white teeth who show you how to put a little backspin on the ball and you say, "Oh, gee, I think I see what you mean, can you show me again," so he'll put his hand on one elbow and stand close, showing you the right grip.

He had a little tray of what looked like test tubes, fluids he poured into the pool, one after another, screwing the caps back on tight. Then he stirred the water with his hand and used the water vacuum to suck up the dirt and dead stuff that sits on the bottom.

The pool looks pretty at first glance, but the grill at the bottom is rusting and black, the chrome flaking off. Sometimes I would go out by the pool and stand there, impatient, like he's wasting my time and I have to be somewhere for supper, like all I want to do is swim my laps and pop into the shower.

He would look at me and say "hi," or "what's up?"

but you could tell he would rather stir chlorine into water than get involved with someone ten years younger than he is. Even when I wore the Day-Glo green two-piece he would just kind of squint at me, as though the sun were behind me and he couldn't see me very well.

His squinty grin made him look wrinkled. If he kept making this expression he'd look as bad as my aunt in a few more years, but I needed to talk. I get that way from my mother, inherited her need to talk, and my dad says I even sound a little like her, although I can't hear this myself. I like excitement, but sometimes I can't shut up.

"Did you always want to work for a pool company?" I said.

He was over by the end of the pool, where the hot water flows out. I was nowhere near the sun, he could see me fine, but he only looked up once. When you're in the pool, you can lean against the hole in the wall and the water wells out and feels like a big muscle working there. He was looking down into the workings of the pool heater, a machine that looked like all those pieces of equipment do, pipes and vents, covered with a little dust.

"I don't work for the company," he said. "I own it."

This did shut me up for a minute, but not because I was impressed. His company logo was the outline of a man carrying a pool on his back, a little-kid-type pool with the water sloshing out. The little man is one of those cartoon figures I can't stand, where the head is very big and the body very small. The name on the little blue pickup was Aquascan, not a bad name, but the pool man must have made up the cartoon all by himself, or maybe picked it out of a graphics catalog.

I had to imagine the pool man, *Yeah, that looks like a good logo; I want to drive around in a truck with that little man with the big head on it.*

"I used to think I wanted to be a teacher," he said. "I wanted to teach chemistry."

I liked chemistry well enough—litmus paper and equations, Mr. Welling handing out quizzes you had to fill in sitting on metal stools, a lab sink and a swan-neck faucet at your elbow. I liked biology a lot more—amoebas and vertebrae.

My dad called the pool man Barry, and he called my dad Mr. Charles, but as usual I realized I didn't know very much about this man. I couldn't just call him Barry. I should call him Mister Something, but that made me feel all the more like someone he wouldn't take seriously.

Now that Barry had begun to look at me straight on, I was glad I was wearing that oversize pool robe my mother brought me from Palm Springs, one of those big hooded robes made of the same stuff towels are made of, so you don't have to dry off; the material soaks up the moisture.

"Your dad be home soon?" he asked.

It was one of those situations where you try to guess what the questioner wants to hear. My dad was lik-able, and when he and the pool man talked they seemed to get along fine, talking about how much water gets lost to evaporation and how much because of microfissures in the pool bottom, cracks no one can see with the naked eye.

But for some reason I had the impression he wanted my dad to not be home, maybe so he could get up the nerve it would take to sit down in one of the pool chairs and have a conversation with me.

"I never know what he's going to do," I said at last.

Now that I had Barry's attention, I didn't want it, and I didn't want to talk about my dad. But there was something about Barry that kept me looking at him, not wanting the conversation to end.

"Are you cold?" said Barry, putting the lid back on the pool heater. He stood on the lid to make sure it was on snug. He was wearing Sperry Top-Siders, the kind with the white soles that keep you from slipping. He wasn't looking at me, coiling the tube of the water vacuum.

"A little," I said.

I could see now what it was about Barry that kept me standing there. His eyes were the color of Adler's eyes, gray, and he was slow and careful, like Adler. Adler talks to me like this, the man who had just married my mother.

My mother got everything she wanted out of life. All she had to do was reach out and take it.

"People think since this is California, they ought to have a pool," Barry was saying.

"I like to swim," I said. He knew all about that. He was always cleaning my hair out of the filter.

"This is what I call soft-core California," he said. "San Francisco, the East Bay, all of it hardly ever gets really warm."

"It's warm enough," I said. Maybe talking to Maureen gets me into the habit of arguing.

"You dad tells me you're going to study pre-law," he said.

"I still have a year of high school," I responded. "My dad was the best student Boalt Law School ever had," I added. "He was in a debate once with the dean of the law school."

"I bet he won the debate."

"Of course. It's famous."

"What was the debate about?"

"It was a joke subject, one of those they pick just to get an argument going. Whether or not the Earth was flat."

Barry gave a little laugh. "Did he prove it was flat?"

"It is."

It was a joke of my own, but he didn't laugh again. He slung the coiled tube over his shoulder.

"Your dad helped me with my business papers," Barry said. "It's a fictitious firm name," he said.

"Aquascan. You have to make sure no other company has the same name—"

"Or maybe there's a Mr. Aquascan," I said, "born with that name, cleaning pools somewhere."

"Right," Barry said. "Otto Aquascan."

"That could be the name of the guy on the truck," I said. "You could call him that." I didn't say *that stupid-looking cartoon figure you picked for your company.*

"What guy?" said Barry, and I could tell I was losing it, the energy going out of the conversation already. It didn't take long, especially with someone older, someone busy, someone who probably had eight girlfriends, all of them with MAs in chemistry. You can only keep their attention and their respect so long, and then something distracts them, they have someplace to go or a call to make.

"Oh, him!" said Barry at last. "My partner picked him out. Otto Aquascan."

"He's cute," I said, which was about the exact opposite of what I really thought. I don't know what happens to my mouth sometimes—it says things and I can't stop it.

"I'm glad you think so." Barry was heading toward the gate, a trickle of water following him from the coiled tube on his shoulder.

All I could think was: I can't stand waiting all by myself for my father to come home and go through the same things we've been through before.

I knew I could explain myself. I simply wanted to fast-forward through this next couple of hours, and get to where my father had worried himself into a state of talked-out exhaustion, and then we'd watch one of his old videos, Marines blowing up castles held by Nazis.

I swam back and forth underwater, the water pressure in my ears hurting a little. Swimming underwater is my favorite exercise, but the fact is I don't swim as often as I should. If I want to lose a little weight I just tend to stop eating for a while.

I took a hot shower, and after I used some of that cologne Mother left when she moved to Oakland, I put on the kind of clothes I used to wear, a full cotton skirt with little orange flowers and an oversize Indonesian cotton blouse, a shirt designed for a man to wear, tiki pattern all over it in purple.

I sat in my bedroom and slipped the scrapbook out of the bottom drawer. It was a secret, and I kept it under an old photo album and a pair of white, gold-trimmed cowgirl boots I had outgrown before junior high.

They were articles by Adler. He writes about why people overeat, why we get headaches. There was an article on bed-wetting, how parents need to reassure children. There was an article I had reread so many times it was coming loose off the page. It was on our dreams, and what it means when we fall in love with someone in a dream, a person we have never seen before.

I put the scrapbook back in the bottom drawer, all the way in the back where no one would see it even if they looked, covered up with a folder of drawings from primary school, my first alphabet.

I needed to talk to Ted. He sends me a message sometimes on the computer and says he's doing okay. That's it for Ted. My brother would rather dig a hole than talk on the telephone. His computer messages are impersonal, but interesting. Once he found a rattlesnake skin with the rattle attached on top of the air conditioner, and he wondered how it got up there, maybe a flying snake.

Dad said Ted was going to be a major success in landscaping, but I knew my dad would never stop wondering why Ted couldn't go to school and turn into a younger version of Dad. He expected us to like what he liked, the same movies, the same cars.

I sat in the living room, waiting to catch Dad on the way in, get it over with, maybe tell him about the scrape in the Mustang's bumper, a detail I had never mentioned. You can play a situation like this several ways, you just have to take your time to deal, like solitaire, make sure every card gets put neatly onto the right pile.

My dad once told me there isn't such a thing as insanity in a medical sense. It's a word lawyers and newspapers use, the insanity defense. You don't hear a doctor saying that one of his patients is completely insane. Or *crazy*. Psychologists don't confer with each other describing a client as *completely crazy*.

It became clear after a while that my dad was not coming home, making me wait, letting me twist on my rope. Maybe he would stay out all night, the way he did sometimes.

When the phone rang, I let the machine answer it. I knew it might be Mom, calling to see if I was okay, but I had a feeling it was Dad, calling to tell me where he was. Every time it rang, I just sat there.

If he wanted me to wait, that's what I would do.

··· 8 ···

Some people keep tapes of sports bloopers, referees slipping, landing on their butts. Some people keep tapes of naked men and women, gasping and sweaty.

Dad keeps videotapes of depositions, people explaining how their lives became empty, lifeless planets. He stores them in a box. He uses them in his law practice—people testifying who, for some reason, can't or won't go before a judge and jury.

I found one tape especially interesting. On this tape a woman tells the story of how her husband, estranged for six months, came home while the live-in maid was away. The husband tried to seize a portrait of her, an oil painting, rip it right off the wall.

Then he tried to force himself on the woman, to use my dad's phrase, but the husband had been drinking, and one thing did not necessarily lead to another. He hurt the woman, falling on top of her, pinching a major nerve. Now she had trouble getting up and walking, gravity too painful for her. She had to testify in a wheelchair in her living room. She wore sparkling black earrings and too much eye makeup.

Sometimes her emotions were so strong she couldn't talk. I watched this tape, waiting for my father to come home. The tape had a halting, authentic feeling to it, a *Court TV* appeal, not at all like a soap, where you know the people are actors and only pretending.

This woman was pretending, too. She was pretending she would be all right someday.

Dad opened the door and came in, briefcase in one hand, keys in the other. He hurried in, just as his voice on the tape was asking the woman to describe the nightmares she had when she finally got to sleep.

He tossed the briefcase onto the sofa. "What are you watching that for?" he said, switching off the television.

I couldn't think of an answer.

"I came home as fast as I could," he said. He was breathless. "My day blew up."

I just sat there. It was late, after nine, but not as late as it could have been.

"I had a horrible day," he said. "I'm all set to go to trial tomorrow, feeling great, and my client goes and does something incredibly stupid. I had the worst day I have had in years."

He noticed I wasn't saying anything. "You got my messages." He looked at me. My dad doesn't look at me often, doesn't look at anyone. He likes to talk while he looks at something else, the parrot fish or the news. But he looked at me now, really seeing me.

I shrugged with one shoulder.

"What happened today?" he said.

He meant: to me, at the department store, and I felt myself teeter on the edge of something. The VCR was still running even though the TV screen was blank, and it made a small electronic hum on the shelf under my dad's war movie collection.

I started to tell him, but everything in my mind shut down. I thought I was going to cry.

"Is this how it's going to be from now on?" he asked.

The only really important thing you learn from a lawyer is when to shut up.

Dad kept talking. "You're going to start stealing things, is that it?"

I looked away. I tried to say *I didn't do it.* No sound came out.

"My career is hamstringing me right now, Anna. I don't have time for anything extra."

I couldn't look at him.

"If you're going to start engaging in criminal behavior, please let me know so I can make some arrangements." He liked talking like this, businesslike and crisp, battling the universe without getting his suit wrinkled.

"I didn't do it," I said, clearly this time.

He thought about this. He paced around a little, pulling at his lower lip.

"I know Jane pretty well," he said at last. "The manager of the store. She and I spent some time together last year." He meant that the manager of I. Magnin was a former girlfriend. He liked to make you work to understand him. It made him a little hard to follow, but it could be fun, playing Ping-Pong with a pro.

"Maybe she's just getting back at me," Dad said. "Needling me. Telling me my daughter's a thief."

I looked away, at the floor, at the high polish on my dad's black shoes. Sometimes when I'm talking to my father, the world vanishes, every city, every other human being. There is nothing but the two of us.

"She said the store made a mistake," Dad was saying. "But she had an attitude, the way she said it. They touched you, right?"

"Sort of."

"Be sure, Anna. This is important."

"Tell me why you're so late."

I almost never talk to my dad so directly, and he sat down, my words pushing him into the recliner. The chair went all the way back, folded out, so his feet were out. He hunched around, trying to get the footrest to tuck back in.

"I left three different messages," he said. "I'm not the one sitting there with eye makeup down my face."

"You don't want to pursue this," I said, using one of his phrases. It's not hard to sound like a lawyer. You didn't want to pursue certain matters when the totality of the situation meant you were acting like a retard.

"It's really between me and Jane," Dad said. "If she and I had never dated, she wouldn't have decided to make a fuss about you. She wanted to embarrass me."

Dated. Dad would come out with a word like that sometimes, as though he were still a teenager in some earlier era. He had *girlfriends* and *blind dates,* a man who defended ex-mayors, talking like he was back in high school.

"She was right." The words popped out of me.

He didn't hear me.

But then he did, realizing what I had said, after a few seconds. He has a face people like, an oddly familiar look. Sometimes I go to a banquet with Dad, Dad wanting to include me in his life, and people whisper to me, *Is he on TV?* And I smile.

His face looks good in photographs. Only in person do you see his gaze moving around while people talk to him.

"You didn't really try to steal anything, did you?" he asked.

I shut up.

He struggled to get out of the chair, and then gave up. He just sat there, looking at the ceiling. "God help me," he said.

I just sat there.

"I can't take it," he said. "I've done all I can. You people are going to tear me apart, one little piece at a time."

He didn't mean *you people.* He meant *you women.*

He meant his clients, his paralegals, his contacts in the media, everybody.

"You're not going to do this to me," he said.

And then I began to talk.

Sometimes my father really listens. It isn't often, but it happens. The two of us have a planet to ourselves.

·· 9 ··

I kept my voice steady. It only took a few minutes. I think I even took a small, bitter pleasure in it. "I pretend I'm stealing things," I said.

I could feel him listening, feel him not wanting to.

My words were a new third person in the room, an intruder. Maybe I had expected him to deny the possibility, insist that it wasn't true.

I said, "I made myself quit."

"Until today," he said. He was out of the chair, beginning to pace the room the way I had expected him to.

I didn't respond.

"You pretend," he said, a half question.

I hate it when my voice comes out sounding like someone who hasn't spoken in ten thousand years. I whispered, "That's right."

"Except today. Today you weren't pretending." My

father got the point too quickly. He couldn't keep from sounding like a lawyer lancing a star witness.

I felt myself going dry inside. "What happened to your client?" I asked.

My question didn't even seem to make sense to him. But then he turned to look at me and he said, "He disappeared."

"The child molester?"

My dad inclined his head a little, not wanting to acknowledge the possible guilt of one of his wealthy clients, and maybe not wanting to discuss child molesters with me in any detail.

"He ran away?" I said.

"The trial begins tomorrow. His wife doesn't know anything. His friends all know nothing. I go to his house, a big place, up in the hills, nice view. The guy's gone."

"Maybe he'll be back."

"I know the signs."

"You can't tell what someone else is doing."

He let himself look at me. "True."

My feelings kept me quiet for a moment.

My dad knows how to keep talking while things settle down emotionally. "He left with snapshots of his wife, his mom and dad. He took funny little things, his grandfather's cuff links, odd keepsakes you want with you when you're never coming back."

He was not pacing, he was just standing, looking at the fish in the aquarium.

There is a loach who lives at the bottom of the fish

tank and feeds on the moss that grows on the sand. He never asked *how is the tang, how is the parrot fish*. It was always: *How is the coolie loach doing?* It was a little fish that was colorless and thoughtful-looking, one of those students who study hard and barely pass. I think he liked it because you had to think before you could see it, figure out where it might be.

"I called you," he said. "I left four or five messages."

I said, "I think Mother left some messages, too."

This stopped him for a second. "Saying what?"

"I didn't listen to them. I just heard her voice saying something over the machine. I didn't play the messages back. She was tense, the way she gets."

I wanted my father to say *I know the way she gets*, a continuing minor conspiracy against her, but he said nothing.

I said, in my talking-fossil voice, "She wanted to know where I was."

He was looking at me so intently I had to look away from him. "There's something else happening here," he said. "Something you're not telling me."

I kept quiet. The aquarium gurgled. Sometimes it sounds pretty, calming. Right now I wanted to dump all the water out all over the floor.

"Is everything okay between you and Stu?"

"I haven't seen him in a couple of weeks."

"Is that what's bothering you?"

You don't have to answer every question. If you don't feel like talking, you can shut up.

"I'm going to tell your mother," he said. "I can't

handle this. It's humiliating, but it's the truth." He glanced at his wristwatch. "I'm calling her now. I'm going to ask her to come over." She lived near Lake Merritt, although she was getting ready to move. She could be here in twenty minutes.

What a mess it would make, water everywhere, fish flopping on the carpet. "Not tonight," I said, my voice sounding awful.

"It's something we have to take care of," he said.

I got up and took his hand. My hand was pale and slender, and his hand was weathered, broad, flat. I wanted to tell him not to call Mother, not now.

He withdrew his hand. He picked up the phone on the piano. One of his shoes knocked lightly against the piano leg, and there was a faint reverberation, a piano string coming briefly to life.

I went into the hall bathroom. Every time the light is switched on a fan starts up. You can't hear anything but an airy whine from the ceiling. The light there wasn't any good, one of the bulbs stuttering. It made shadows jump up and down on my face as I washed myself and shook my head so my hair fell back into place. I wondered where Ted got electricity, all the way out on the desert.

Ted had said I could come and see him, marvel at the sun and the sand, or some other half-bookish, half-joking Ted phrase like that, the complicated directions written on a postcard.

I joined my father again. He was off the phone. Whatever he had said, it had taken very little time.

"But how would you do that?" I said, standing next

to my father, both of us looking into the aquarium.

"Do what?" asked my dad, half-lost in his own thoughts.

"Disappear," I said.

"Don't use credit cards," he said, not paying much attention. "Use only cash. And don't get any speeding tickets." Then he stopped himself, looking at me, thinking about what he had just said.

··· 10 ···

I was surprised, and slumped against the fridge.

I had expected my mother, but not Adler, too. When I heard his voice, I wanted to slip out the back door and never come back.

It was late, after ten, and I was starving, except I knew I wouldn't be able to eat. I tore the endpaper off a new roll of Tums. I leaned against the refrigerator, trying to hear what they were saying.

She didn't want to see me, either. You could hear it in the house, the way the two men had audible voices but my mother's voice was quiet. You couldn't hear her when she spoke, but you knew she was talking by the silence of the other voices.

They talked for a long time. I boiled some water and added some spaghetti, and when the spaghetti was done I poured it out into the colander in the sink. I like the way the steam feels in my face and the way the kitchen windows get fogged for a minute or two, although the steam makes my hair stick out funny.

I opened the back door to let some of the steam out and I thought: Escape.

Go ahead and run.

At the cooking class at Redwood School I always thought it was fun to make cocoa from scratch, a little brown powder with that wonderful smell, a little NutraSweet, stirring all the time while you add the hot milk. Maybe that would be a good plan later on, I thought, cocoa for everybody.

But then she was there in the kitchen doorway.

She stood with her arms crossed. She was wearing black pumps that made her look too tall, her hair frosted with gold highlights, and some kind of new color around her eyes, professionally done.

She didn't smile, she didn't not-smile, she just looked. "I spent a long afternoon at Nordstrom's." Then she added, "Your father explained what happened."

God knows, I thought, what mangled version of events he managed to tell. I suppose I made some kind of sign that I heard her.

"I'm not the confused person I used to be," she said. "I know how to share my life, Anna. If you let me."

"I'm sorry about today," I said.

My voice was quiet, and Mother had to turn her head to hear me.

"We've been doing better recently, you and I," she said.

"I was looking forward to shopping with you," I said. I had more to say, a little, truthful speech, but I couldn't go on.

She and I had fought terribly when I was fourteen, and my father had suggested keeping me here, close to my school. She didn't know my daily habits anymore, what I liked to wear, what kind of cereal I liked in the morning, but little by little we had been spending more time together.

She left the kitchen doorway. I thought for a moment she was going to walk in, give me a hug, give the steaming pasta a toss, but instead she turned and left me alone in the brightly lit room.

Staging is everything with her. She was letting me make my entrance. She had started out as an assistant director, making sure guests in the control room stayed quiet when the director was working, changing from camera one to the floor shot on camera four.

She had machine-gunned her way to the top, and now she fired sportscasters and had the parking-lot fence topped with coiled barbed wire. Channel Two News had gotten three awards in the last year.

I didn't want to look his way, but I did. Adler was on the blue leather sofa, his gray eyes making him look like someone who would understand anything I would ever do. He wore a dark wool sports jacket, Italian cut, with a navy blue tie, and sometimes when other people were talking he would put his hand on the knot of his tie. Adler moves slowly and likes to touch things, make sure they are still there.

Dad sat there with his hands cupped like someone praying, except he wasn't praying. He was looking at his ex-wife's back, or maybe even her butt, but it wasn't a sexy look.

"There have to be some changes," said Mother. She had been in therapy for three years with a woman and had gone to self-help seminars, where she had met Adler.

"I made some pasta," I said.

"We are going to help you," she said, with her smile, arms crossed, fingers clenching the sleeves of her red suit jacket. Sometimes Mom wears too much makeup. When you do that, your face looks good, but your hands look old.

"I don't want to talk about it," I said. When in doubt ask for a continuance. "I made plenty of spaghetti, the imported kind."

Then she really surprised me. She cried. Not much, but there was a definite wetness in her eyes. Mother didn't cry very often. I saw at that moment how much Adler had helped her. I saw how lucky she was.

"You want my attention," she said, walking away. She didn't look in my direction when she added, "You need me."

Mother was doing this partly because she had an audience, but partly because she meant it. Adler looked at me and gave me one of his smiles, a wise man who never failed to marvel at people like my mother. He was a psychologist, and he had been in

Vietnam, Mother told me once, and had seen terrible things.

The wedding had been a month before, quick: flowers, an overweight photographer. After months of talking it had happened, and I had been there. Maureen had come down to Carmel, too, telling me her shoes were killing her about nine hundred times. I hadn't held flowers or anything like that. I had worn an uncomfortable robin's-egg blue satin, a dress that sounded like fir trees in the wind every time I moved, not a good thing if you're not a fir tree.

"We'll be back in a week," she said. "When we come back, we want you to move in with us in our new house in San Francisco."

Dad looked at me, looked at Adler, looked at the floor, his eyes always moving. His silence made it clear: *We* included him.

My brain made me not understand for a moment.

"For the rest of the summer," said Adler, the first time he had spoken, the sound of his voice causing my mother to turn and look at him. "It's a nice, big house. You can see the sailboats."

Dad saw the look in my eyes. He said, "I really can't help you anymore." My father looked at the wall, looked at his hands.

We had been in family counseling at Kaiser for a few months when Mother moved out. Dad had said at the time that Mother was afraid of her own adulthood.

Mother turned her head, thinking I had said something. A cherry bomb had blown up near her left ear when she was eight years old. I realized for the millionth time that she was too proud to wear a hearing aid in her dead ear. I wanted to protect her from danger, from me.

Sometimes when I was little, we took naps together. I would wake up first and lie next to her listening to her breathing. Sometimes her feet would twitch, and I thought: She's having a dream. She's running in the dream.

Adler gave me one of his looks, his peaceful eyes, which had seen men die.

Everyone said they had already eaten. My dad and I would have enough spaghetti to feed Eastern Europe.

I stood in the darkness while my mother got into her Saab. Adler opened the passenger door, the inside of the car instantly full of light. "Don't be so anxious, Anna." I couldn't see his face, only his hand holding out some offering he could not make in words. "We all want to help you."

I thought for a moment he wanted me to take his hand. And I almost did. I took a step toward him across the dark grass.

But I stopped myself and said something ordinary, wishing them a good trip. It was like hearing someone else talk, a voice on a radio.

They left, and I turned to see my father holding open the front door, a black cutout figure.

··· 11 ···

Swimming underwater there is nothing left of the world, and every human voice is filtered. There is only the body, breasts and knees brushing the bottom of the pool, and the feeling that life is burning away in the lungs. I love it, but Stu is right—I should run more.

I woke up very early the next morning. My dreams had been terrible, each one frantic—late for classes, late for a play I was starring in, late for airplanes that were already on the runway. I dreamed I was in a pool, unable to reach the surface.

I made the bed the way they make them in motels, tucked in all around, tight. I put on my fuchsia sweatpants. They have deep front pockets and are baggy, loose in a way that makes you feel naked inside the fabric. I bound my hair back with a rubber band, the band pulling at my hair and hurting a little.

I laced up the running shoes while I sat on the front porch. It was so early the newspapers were being delivered, a green van rolling slowly up the street, rolled-up newspapers firing out of the van as it made its way, a paper hitting a front door with a *thwack*. An Asian man on the passenger's side saw me or I probably would have had to duck. The paper slapped the steps at my feet, and I let it lie.

There were sow bugs. They rolled up when I touched them, and tickled my fingers with their tiny legs. My mother had chosen the welcome mat at

Payless Hardware years ago, black rubber spikes for taking mud off the shoes, the word *welcome* in red.

Running makes me cough.

It also makes me sweat, and I hate that. After a short time I was walking, the morning sunlight on the dewy grass. Sometimes another jogger would huff by on the other side of the street, and sometimes there would be someone doing exer-walking, an out-of-shape person striding along with weights in his hands.

Some people don't seem to realize the battle is hopeless, they are just out of shape and they might as well quit. Ted says we can be whatever we want to be, but I can't see it. I don't believe in plastic surgery, either, and I think that when you get old, keeping yourself pretty by going to the surgeon is like athletes taking drugs so they can jump hurdles.

But it was nice to be away from the house, and away from my father, who was probably up by now, watching the news and making his breakfast Power Shake: milk and banana and vitamin powder.

A few early risers leaned on walls and telephone poles on Solano Avenue, caffeine addicts outside the coffee places there, and they looked bad. They were baggy-eyed and their hair was messed up, the women looking worse than the men, puffy and tired-looking.

The redwood tree in the parking lot of Andronico's grocery store was full of birds, as usual, but as usual I couldn't see any. I could only hear them, and maybe once in a while there would be a flutter, a bird looking for a new perch.

The morning was cool and cloudy, the way it often is in the summer. A couple of the men gave me one of their looks, but I gave them each a look right back that pretty much took the light out of their eyes. I did manage to run a little bit when I looped back to Colusa and made it back to Capistrano.

I stopped there, wanting to cry out. A deer was bounding down the middle of the street.

Deer are supposed to be quiet creatures, but this one made a sound, each hoof crisp on the asphalt. The deer curved its front legs, arching them prettily, and for a moment the animal didn't seem in a hurry, jogging beautifully down the middle of Capistrano Street, heading in the wrong direction, down into the neighborhood, away from the hills.

The deer was running gingerly because it was uncertain. There were houses and parked cars everywhere, and a dog was gaining on it.

It was a dark dog, trailing a leash, its tongue out. I could hardly recognize the animal in its intensity.

It was Lincoln. I called out his name but he didn't glance at me as he passed. He did make a long, exhaled sniff without slowing, a minimal *hello*, a friend too rapt to stop.

I had never seen a dog chase a deer, but I had a clear sense of what would happen next.

The dog would corner the deer. Lincoln would trap the deer against a wall and tear it up. I don't know where the thought came from but it was there, as though my genes knew more about this than my own memory—the big dog would tear the deer to pieces.

I screamed. This was not a Hollywood, fright-night scream. This was a huntress's command. The sound of my voice did seem to slow Lincoln for an instant. I could see him stiffen, hearing me. A flash of apology passed through him. Then he rounded the corner and vanished.

Maybe the deer would fight back. Maybe he would hook Lincoln with one of the antlers. That was a painful thought, too, and I was sprinting hard, around the corner and up, following the two animals.

I lost them. Somewhere in the maze of gardens and garages the dog and the deer were running, and I was frantic, calling out the dog's name.

Until there was nothing to do but give up and walk back, feeling beaten. A woman crept down her front steps in a pink bathrobe, her hand holding on to the rail beside the steps. She wore hair rollers, her hair up under a kerchief. A man watered his lawn, careful so only a little water darkened the redwood chips bordering the grass.

People really don't see much, don't care much about the things that happen. Maybe it's hard enough for them to get up out of bed every morning, another day.

There was Lincoln, coming back down Capistrano, just like the first time, but wet with his own saliva, now, panting. I hurried after the dog, but this time when I called breathlessly Lincoln slowed, and turned to look as I snatched at the leash and caught it.

Lincoln jumped up and down, breathing hard. My

hand slipped and I had to hang on tight. I got a better grip, Lincoln testing my strength, experimenting with the power of the leash.

I gave the leather strap a few good turns around my wrist. Lincoln gave a half-spoken yowl, telling me to let him go. The leash was taut, the dog begging me, good-humored, but feinting, lunging.

··· 12 ···

Maureen's father was getting on his bicycle when I panted up the front lawn with Lincoln.

It's an old bike, but Mr. Dean rides it every morning to the campus in Berkeley, a black-and-white three speed that creaks. He stood there with one leg up on the bike and closed his eyes and opened them. "Thank God," he said.

Lincoln had his tail between his legs.

"Anna, I was in a panic. I can't run, not like you. I was going off on my bike to look." He gave a little laugh. "Maureen's off looking for Lincoln at Indian Rock. Once he went up there and ran around making a nuisance. Lincoln, where were you?"

Lincoln hung his head, wagging his tail experimentally. I told Mr. Dean about the deer.

"Oh, that's not good at all, not at all," said Mr. Dean.

He gave a little laugh. "It's my fault. It's my fault, Lincoln," he said to the dog. "One day I was going to go to Petland and get one of those big chains, the stainless steel ones. I took a look at one of those, and I said, 'Lincoln doesn't need a chain like that, not a dignified dog like Lincoln.'"

Maureen sprinted down the street, and when she reached us, bent over, her hands on her knees. "I can't breathe," she said finally. "I'm going to die."

"Lincoln almost did a terrible thing," said Mr. Dean. He made his laugh, a small karate chop of a chuckle. "He almost caught a deer. Isn't that right, Lincoln? A deer for breakfast." He spoke to the dog in a normal speaking voice, not in a little cute voice, the way some people talk to animals.

Lincoln looked at me, sniffed the lawn, not meeting Mr. Dean's eyes. I thought the dog was exaggerating his feeling of shame a little, but a person or an animal can exaggerate and still be sincere.

"It shows how little we know." He made his laugh again. Mr. Dean's laugh has nothing to do with anything seeming funny. It's a nervous sound he makes in the middle of his sentences. Mr. Dean talks like a very nervous man being questioned by the police and trying to carry it off. He might tell you terrible news and still make his little laugh: An earthquake—*heh*—has destroyed Los Angeles.

Mr. Dean found a rope under the house, a big gray rope like something you might use to tie up a bull. The rope had been under the house awhile and was dirty with dead moths and what looked like daddy longlegs

legs. Mr. Dean worked the big rope through the loop in the choke collar and tied Lincoln to a tree.

"Is that what we need, Lincoln?" said Mr. Dean. "A whale rope?" He gave Lincoln his orange dish full of water, and Lincoln gave us all a kind look, as though the dog understood our limitations.

Mrs. Dean was in Spokane on business, and Mr. Dean and Maureen heated some Sara Lee cherry strudel. We sat there in the dining room. Maureen looked pink-cheeked from her run, and everyone was happy, now that Lincoln was back safe. Mr. Dean told a story about a dog he used to know that would slink away whenever you put your hands up to your eyes like you were holding binoculars.

"Or like this," said Mr. Dean, curving his forefingers, like someone pretending to wear glasses. "The poor dog would hate it when people did that. He hid behind the couch."

"We had a parakeet who would fall off his perch when I wore a baseball cap," said Maureen.

"Birds panic," said Mr. Dean. Mr. Dean wears the same suit every day, a gray business suit with a vest. He was wearing it today, with a bow tie, the bicycle clips he uses on his pantlegs beside his coffee cup.

I couldn't believe that Maureen could be sitting here talking to her father so cheerfully. Maybe they hadn't discussed the shattered vase. Maybe Mr. Dean didn't know about it, and I even turned to look at the bare space on the shelf, wondering if Maureen had sneaked another art object into its place. She hadn't.

Sometimes I am so sure I know what a person or an

animal is feeling. Other times I can't tell what people are thinking, as though they have taken a sudden off-ramp and I'm rolling along alone, no one else in sight.

Walking past a row of clay objects, I thought I might start breaking them one by one, starting with the blue frog.

··· 13 ···

There are very few pets in Petland, just a few yellow-green parakeets sitting in their cages with their black eyes looking around at nothing. There are sacks of songbird seed and great bunches of millet, and pigs' ears in a big basket, *Smoke-flavored—dogs love 'em*.

Maureen hefted a bright chain and let it fall to the counter. We were the first customers of the day. The cash register had to be unlocked with a little key on one of those coiled plastic springs people wear to keep lucky charms and keys right at their hip. There was only one clerk, and she didn't even bother to glance my way. A shop like this would be easy, if you wanted to steal catnip mice.

"You told him," I said.

"Yeah, I told him," said Maureen, counting out some money.

Maureen didn't take a bag. She wrapped the chain around her arm like a gladiator.

"What did he say?" I asked when we were outside.

"He said it was an accident."

The chain slipped from her arm, glittering, and fell to the sidewalk. She picked it up.

"I'm going to pay him back for it," she said.

I thought about this. "How much did it cost?" I asked, but Maureen just looked at me with a smile that meant: I didn't get the point.

When Maureen is happy, she makes everyone around her happy. She swung the new dog chain and danced a little as we made our way up Colusa. Maureen is one of those people who can hear music in their heads, listening to songs they remember without even humming, even dancing to those tunes if she feels like it. For some reason I was suddenly sick of her.

"You don't even know how to walk," I said.

"Shut up." Nice, too happy to take me seriously.

"Look at you, all over the sidewalk." Maureen prefers guys who are just as unformed as she is, baggy, worn-out clothes and vague habits, people who can sleep all day and then jump up and down with excitement because a team on television just scored.

She stopped doing arabesques up the sidewalk, although she rolled her eyes at me like she was doing me a huge favor.

"When you walk," I said, "you shouldn't let all your weight go down on one foot, and then take another step and let all your weight down on that foot. That's not walking. That's lumbering."

"At least I don't mince."

"You walk like a cavewoman," I said. "It's embarrassing."

My jogging clothes were loose and comfortable. I just walked along, showing Maureen how to stay centered.

My father was on the phone, pacing up and down in front of the aquarium. CNN was on with the sound off, someone getting out of a car, not talking, heading into a courthouse.

Dad tossed the phone onto the sofa when he was done with it, and hitched at his pants, looking at me, and then looking up at the ceiling. He was wearing a summer-weight suit, butterscotch yellow. His shoes were London tan, and his tie was toast brown, everything more or less matching, colors that made him look tired.

"We have a week," he said, staying where he was.

"Six days," I said. "They leave for Canada in forty-five minutes."

I love details. You can say you'd like to scream, or you can say you'd like to hit high C above the treble clef. Mother and Adler were on flight 709 out of SFO.

He said, "Your mother's very concerned. So am I."

"What are they going to do up there, feed bears? Mother doesn't even like the beach because sand gets in her shoes."

"They have a nice hotel up there, Lake Louise. Very comfortable, very pretty. Your mother and I went there when we'd been married maybe a year." He didn't want to talk about that. "You went jogging?"

"Something different," I said.

"I want you to do something with your time," he said.

I could almost feel sorry for him, a man women liked, having trouble talking to his own daughter. "Such as?"

"Something safe."

"Something that won't get your name in the news," I said. I regretted saying it. He blinked and walked over to the aquarium.

"Windsurfing," I heard him say. "Riding lessons. Volunteer at Legal Aid."

I was surprised at what I said next. "Why does Adler like Mother, anyway? What does he see in her?"

He was shaking food into the aquarium, holding a container like a pepper shaker, sprinkling Vitablend into the water. He gave me one of his best deadpan attorney looks. "Your mother's a lovely woman," he said.

"Do I remind you of her? Is that why you can't stand me?" I meant this breezily, but it came out too blunt.

"You have so much promise," he said. There was something in his voice, a little rasp of feeling, that touched me.

I wanted to ask him if he thought I really *did* resemble my mother. If I resembled her emotionally, I was in for years of domestic hurricane. I wanted to ask him what he thought of Adler, but I couldn't bring myself to utter his name.

I wanted to tell him there was no way I could live in the same house with my mother and Adler.

I left my jogging clothes in a heap, took a shower, tried to read a book Maureen had liked, about a blind man coming home after a war, happiness and suffering, all colorful feelings, signs of intelligent life.

That afternoon I had the tank filled at the Chevron on Solano Avenue, sitting in the full-service bay and asking the guy to please check the fluid levels and the tires. I was the best student in auto shop, not being afraid to look up at the gearbox from inside the auto bay, down underneath the car where bits of caked grease fall on you and get in your hair.

All the while I tried to forget that I was the same person of just the day before. I tried to forget, and I succeeded.

For a while.

·· 14 ··

I dropped by Whole Earth, the computer warehouse off Sixth Street where Stu works. I dressed like someone hunting for work, a linen skirt, wicker brown, and a linen top, a cornflower blue the woman at Maxi's called it. It was a nice blue, like the blue in the U.S. flag, only a little more pale. I carried a leather purse exactly the color of caramel. My aunt had sent it to me, and for once I liked one of her presents.

I timed it so I caught Stu on his lunch break. One look at him and I saw why I had liked him. Even eating a jumbo burrito he looked good.

He went to fling his arm around me and I stepped back. "Want a bite?" he said.

I surprised myself by biting off a little flour tortilla and some refritos and a little sour cream.

I looked good enough for Stu to want to be seen with me, and he glanced around the computer storeroom, but there was no one there but a heavy, bearded guy with a box cutter, slicing up boxes and stacking them.

"Need me to show you how to set anything up?" asked Stu. He had that smile, smart, easy to like. "We stand behind all our equipment."

"Assistant Manager," I said, fingering his badge. "That's new."

"Give me six months and I'd be running this place," said Stu.

He crumpled up the burrito wrapper and bounced it off the rim of the trash can. It fell in. Stu was fun and good-looking, and bragged in a way you knew he only half-believed.

We both knew he wouldn't be here six months. He was going to Cal Poly in San Luis Obispo in September, majoring in some sort of science fiction math, three hundred miles away. We both knew how bad we both were at picking up the phone. Stu was complete and liked himself, a life-supporting planet.

"You're looking for trouble," said Stu. He was joking, the way he does, everything about Stu a sort of easy banter.

"No more than usual," I said.

"Then someone better be careful."

I shrugged, acting the way I knew Stu liked me to act, teasing, mocking everything, the way he did. Stu never wanted to talk about what he called the Time Wasters, God or death or fate. He said life was all accident.

"How about tonight?" he said, not having to make any preliminary conversation, leaning back against a stack of boxes. "Take the Mustang up to the view. See what develops."

I knew what he meant by the view, and it wasn't just a view of the Bay and the city lights. I used to think it was wonderful, the way he was so casual about everything.

"I'll pick you up about eight," I said, although I hadn't really intended to say anything of the kind.

He looked happy, but a little thoughtful, maybe hoping we could go to Just Desserts for fudge cake, or maybe see a movie. "Are you all right, Anna?" He gave me a look like he cared, and like he was puzzled by something, as though my mind was a computer program that wasn't turning itself off and on the way it was supposed to.

"Don't they need some more help around here?" I said. "Maybe someone to watch the doors, make sure people only take out what they paid for." I bumped him with my hip as I turned to leave. "Someone could walk right in and help themselves," I said.

I indicated an open box full of Styrofoam noodles, the tops of smaller boxes, imprinted with *Nikon*, barely covered by the packing stuff. I looked back at Stu and his expression was bad, worried and unsure. There was a carton of Pentax binoculars. One of those would fit in one hand, lightweight.

I told myself that Stu was just nervous, here on the job, assistant manager, acting like he invented wiring. Besides, Stu didn't really know me that well, even after all this time.

"What are all these boxes?" I asked, to change the subject.

"Cameras, binoculars. Computer displays." His tone said: You know very well what these things are.

"You have to know how everything works, right? How to hook up the tab to the slot." If I'd had gum in my mouth I would have blown a bubble and popped it at him, acting dumb and having fun.

He stepped across the concrete floor until he had me by the arm, gently. He walked me to the sliding door, open just wide enough for a person to slip through.

I hurt him a little with the door, tugged it shut just a little as he was about to kiss me on my cheek or my ear, whatever he could get his mouth on.

"God, Anna, watch out," he said, rubbing his elbow. "You just about broke my arm."

I gave him a bored look: Hey, what's an arm.

But Stu didn't laugh, following behind me, leaning on the car to look at me when I sat at the steering wheel. He was about to say something serious. "Are you okay?" he asked finally.

"Why? Do I look weird?" I realized that maybe I had

been looking for a job in the back of my mind, hoping that Stu would hand me an application or at least introduce me to someone.

He glanced away, trying to give me a truthful answer.

"You have burrito on your mouth," I said.

It wasn't true.

Driving up Sacramento Street, I pulled over to the side, the brakes whining. Traffic flowed by. I was cold, sick, sure of something bad.

I couldn't bring myself to look in my purse. I knew what I would find there.

Don't look in the purse.

My heart skipped. A police car was there in the rearview, a policeman walking up to me in the side mirror. That meant I would need my driver's license. It was in the purse, where I didn't want to look. Or maybe this was why the police were here. Stu had called them.

The policeman was right outside, tan uniform and dark glasses, a bright brass star, BERKELEY POLICE. I rolled the window down as far as I could, which wasn't far. I could feel the pulse in my throat.

I had tried to lie to myself. I had told myself I was going to have a perfectly normal day.

I couldn't remember taking them, but I knew: There was a new pair of Pentax binoculars in the purse.

··· 15 ···

I tried to open the car door, shoving hard. It stuck, and it took all my strength.

The policeman helped, pulling from his side. He was smiling, one of those officers trying to give the police a good name. He had a nice smile, and a short mustache, a V of white T-shirt showing at his collar. "Just checking to make sure you're okay," he said.

"Is there anything wrong?" I asked.

His partner loomed behind the car, hands on his hips. "You pulled over so suddenly," said the smiling cop.

"Suddenly?" I echoed. Be careful, I warned myself. You sound stupid. Worse than that—you sound frightened. You sound guilty.

"A little erratically," he said.

Police are visitors from another galaxy, a galaxy where no one forgets. Computers store the names of people who have done wrong. Cops know things just by looking. I felt color seep from my clothes, from my body. I was transparent. This man could see into me, and see the unsteady, nervous creature that lived inside me.

I was taking too long to say something reassuring, standing there blinking in the bland afternoon sunlight. My best hope was that I would appear abashed, flustered. Cars were slowing down, passengers taking a look.

Everything imaginable seemed to be hanging from his belt. A billy club with an extra handle sticking out of the side, keys, handcuffs, and other things I couldn't see from the front. And, of course, a handgun.

"I'm sorry," I said at last. I kept my voice soft, nice. I reassured myself that I wasn't in trouble. Not yet. "I thought I forgot something," I said. "I'm not quite used to driving this car."

"We might as well see your driver's license," he said.

He was still smiling. Each cop must learn to do this at some point, I thought. His face was a mask, friendly, but in an impersonal way. If he had to arrest me, he would still be nice. People were looking as they rolled past, observing my little moment of theater. When the policeman saw my hesitation he said, "There's no infraction involved."

No infraction. The words barely sounded like English to me. I knew it was a variety of good news, though. I tugged open the door. I pulled my purse from the passenger's seat. I gathered my nerve. I told myself to go ahead, open the purse and get it over with. The police weren't going to know the difference. Doesn't everyone carry a pair of binoculars with their lipstick?

I opened the purse.

There was lip gloss, wads of Kleenex, a Princess Marcella Borghese kohl pencil, and some Max Factor mascara. My Ray-Bans were folded around a mirror with a koa-wood frame, another gift from my aunt. There was a Bic pen and a snap wallet, some Tums, and a rhinoceros-head eraser. I unsnapped the wallet, slipped the license out of its holder.

There was no pair of binoculars. I leaned against the car.

The policeman thanked me and told me to drive carefully. I thanked him for his help.

I drove very carefully, twenty-five miles an hour all the way home.

There was nothing wrong with me. I had to calm down, and not lurch around in traffic like a maniac.

I was glad to get home. I parked under a tree, in the shade.

We have a two-story house, and we keep it the way it was when Mother lived here. There are pictures on the wall only Mother liked, gray people playing blue lutes, but we leave them up, straightening them when they start to hang a little crooked.

Tina, the housekeeper, comes in a few times a week, washes, folds, cooks, freezes, and then vanishes. Once I saw her wallet when she was looking to see if she had enough change for the bus, smiling children and smiling adults, a complicated family life. Dad says she walks in on little cat feet, and even when she's around you forget about her, one of those short, still people who eventually kill everyone with gopher poison.

She makes me nervous. I suspect she is quietly disapproving of something about me, who knows what. I fold my dirty clothes, put them in the hamper like clothes in a suitcase, and don't like to leave dirty dishes in the sink, signs that we eat and have lives.

Talking to the policeman had convinced me that I was going to have to straighten out my life. That's all I had to do. Just a little mental housekeeping, that's all.

I would start with a little real, hands-on housekeeping, cleaning up my room. It was wonderful to have something to do, dirty socks to bunch up, old magazines to put in a pile.

I was cleaning up, picking up the book about the mustard gas and the guy going back home, saying hello to people in his neighborhood, hearing them say hello back in a strained way. Sometimes you can only tell that you have something really wrong with you by how your friends act. I would hate to be blind.

I was getting two pimples at the corner of my mouth, a mother pimple and a baby. I kept looking into the mirror and hating my bad luck, but there they were. I dabbed some flesh-colored concealer on them, but that made them look even worse.

I was folding up my fuchsia jogging outfit, thinking I should get one in some other shade, not red, because it fades so fast. I felt something in one of the deep pockets.

My hand slipped into the pocket and came out with something hard and gleaming, a blue object with painted-on eyes. At another time the thing would have looked cute. The thing did not belong here, trespassing in my room.

It was true that I had no memory of hiding it in my pocket. But I knew exactly how it had found itself there, and why it was in my hand at that moment. It was a part of Maureen's father's collection of exotic art.

The ceramic frog did not warm in my hand, the way so many things do, picking up body heat. It stayed cold.

··· 16 ···

I sat in my room, a figurine safe in a big doll's house.

I arrayed my Tuscan tabac eye shadow and my Amalfi sunrise overblush and the long blue Princess Borghese eye accent pencil, and touched up my face, working carefully, thinking about Stu and the way he would feel me all over, inside and out, and it was like I was the clothes and he was the human, trying me on for size. I kept screwing up, one eye looking like Elizabeth Taylor in *Cleopatra*.

I put my hand into my ballet slippers, and there it was, the blue frog with its fake eyes. In real life the hunters kill the frogs, dry the skins, and season their arrowheads with the frog powder.

Right now Mother and Adler were probably in a rented car, air-conditioned, although they probably didn't need it. They would be arriving late at the hotel, probably, their room waiting, with maybe an ice bucket of Mother's favorite champagne, Mumm, the French kind, not the kind from Napa.

It was night, and there were trees.

Stu put his hand on my breast, and his touch was warm. I turned away, though. We were done, and I didn't want him touching me anymore.

It was like when we first used to come up here. We would look at the view, the glitter, the tiny movement of cars, from our private place behind the environmental control unit, all to ourselves.

We were up behind the Lawrence Hall of Science in the dark, the concrete space-age buildings looking hopeful and out-of-date. The lights of Berkeley were a cluster of whites and yellows, and then there was the Bay, darkness.

"You act like my mom before the doctor took her off those pills," said Stu.

"What kind of pills," I said, not even bothering to make my voice sound like I was asking a question, just hitting the ball back.

"They made her like a robot."

"Thanks."

He zipped himself up, partway. It got stuck. "The thing I always liked about you—you weren't ordinary."

He was trying to be nice, but he was using the past tense. "That's a blazing compliment." I sounded like someone who was bothered by nothing.

"You used to tell me about funny things you saw on the news," he said.

"It takes someone like me to make plane crashes and massacres sound funny." I couldn't see him very well. He was up on one arm, looking down at me.

The environmental control unit was a squat concrete abutment with metal slotted vents. Hot air flowed out of it with a quiet hum, a big fan circulating the air from the buildings in the distance. The fan was suddenly silent, and the quiet startled both of us for a moment.

"You used to laugh," Stu said, but the feeling was gone from his voice. "You used to tell me what you saw in your dad's trials, imitate witnesses."

It was an unspoken understanding between Stu and me that I was going to be a lawyer and he was going to design space labs. I started to cry, I couldn't help it.

"Are you all right, Anna?"

I almost told him—really talked to him.

"Just because I'm going away doesn't mean we'll be out of touch," he said. "We're still friends." He said something about E-mail and how there weren't any places anymore, how every place was one point on the plane. Distance didn't matter.

"What kind of person am I?" I asked.

The question made him think. "A very interesting person," he said, picking his words carefully.

I wanted to ask him: Am I a thief?

I wanted to ask him: Can you look into my eyes and see my mind dying?

Instead he sounded shaken that I cared so much, not understanding me at all. He was talking about computer modems. He was saying he would write letters. He thought I was going to miss him. I felt sorry for him. I pinched his nose and gave it a little twist.

We used to rent Three Stooges videos and watch them while Stu's parents were in Europe, and it was a routine between us, grabbing an ear or a nose and saying *Why, you* in that sadistic mean-kid way.

"Your dad'll send you away to college," he said. He made himself sound optimistic. "Life will be wonderful."

I like the way we simplify the world when we want to cheer someone up. *Life* and *wonderful,* balloon-size, Disneyland words. Stu was worried that he was responsible for me needing Kleenex, blowing my nose.

I said, "I'm afraid."

"Reality's confusing," said Stu. He considered his words and must have recognized how pointless he sounded. "A state of flux," he added. We were veering into areas Stu didn't like to discuss. He was going to talk about the laws of thermodynamics, telling me that systems devolve, that chaos is at war with structure.

"Have you ever been to Banff?" I asked.

Stu didn't even know where it was.

··· 17 ···

My dad was on the phone.

I could tell as soon as I was through the front door. He was talking to one of his girlfriends, wandering the house, phone to his ear. He was using his special sexy voice, reassuring, warmhearted.

I tried to shut the door quietly. I stood still, right where I was, eavesdropping. He was telling someone everything would be all right. He was telling someone what a wonderful person she was. "You're an exceptional human being," he said to the person on the phone.

But he had heard the front door shut, despite my efforts, and it was crimping his style. He put his head around a corner and said he'd call right back.

He put the phone down in the dining room. Then he

stood looking at me with his hands on his hips, the way one of the policemen had looked at me, blank.

"Where were you?" he asked.

"Out with Stu." I flung myself into his chair, the big recliner. I picked up the mail off the side table. There was nothing for me.

"Leave a note next time," he said.

"I thought I'd be back before you were. As usual."

"Did you eat anything?"

"A little cold spaghetti before I went out." It was still in the fridge, a large cold brain of pasta.

He sat in a dark, wooden piece of furniture, an antique, like a chair's skeleton. My mother had bought it when I was in preschool, light-years ago. "Did you have a good time with Stu?" my dad said.

"Stu's a lot of fun."

He didn't know how to take this. He took his hand-held tape recorder out of an inner pocket. He ran it fast-forward, the voices high-pitched. It might be someone confessing to raping his own daughter, and there his voice would be, sounding like a demented rat.

He got to the place he wanted in the tape. I had the oddest feeling that he wanted to record our conversation. I experienced that shiver of self-consciousness I often feel when someone pulls out a camera.

He put the recorder down on a leather folder at his side. He had work to do that had nothing to do with me.

"I'm thinking of going with you, like we used to as a family." When he saw that I didn't know what he was talking about, he said, "Kaiser Hospital, family counseling. If you want me to."

Poor man. Orbiting some distant legal sun. "I don't think it would do any good," I said.

"You might as well express it, Anna."

I thought: He can read your mind.

"Express what?" I heard myself say.

"Your anger with me."

"Am I angry with you?" I wasn't being coy—I didn't know what my lines were supposed to be.

"You should be." He took a moment, getting ready to say it. "I'm not much of a father."

This was painful. The look in his eyes, the roughness in his voice. He had it all backwards.

Or maybe he expected reassurance. Maybe the recorder was turned on after all, and he hoped to get my voice on tape: No, you're a wonderful dad. I'm not surprised so many women fall in love with you.

The chair fought with me. I could not climb out of it. My skirt got hiked up, and I felt like one of those photos you see, an actress getting out of a limo, struggling.

My father looked away, maybe not wanting to see his daughter with her skirt up over her face. I was finally out of the chair, and I felt like kicking it.

The aquarium gurgled, and a vague, colorless creature, the coolie loach, crept out from around a ceramic rock. My father followed my gaze and got up to peer into the aquarium.

"How are your fluid levels?" he asked, not looking at me.

"I had them topped up," I said. He was referring to the car. Sometimes you need a manual to understand what Dad is trying to say.

"Have them use nondetergent forty-weight," he said. He turned to see if I was still there and I saw a strange expression in his eyes, wonderment, worry, as though he saw me for the first time after a long trip somewhere, as though I was descending from an airplane instead of climbing the stairs to my room. "An older car like that can overheat," he said. "You could have a real problem."

I continued up the stairs.

"What did you do today?" he asked.

I stood at the top of the stairs. I could only see his shiny black shoes. "I almost got a traffic ticket," I said. "But I didn't."

He stepped to the foot of the stairs, where I could see all of him, looking up at me. "Did you talk your way out of it?" he asked. He would like that, the two of us with the same natural talent.

There was a moment when we enjoyed each other. "Maybe I did," I said.

I could see him thinking that this was good. I could talk my way out of trouble. I had a future.

Then I added, "Do you really think I'll be happier living with Mother?" And Adler, I didn't say. With Mother and Adler in their new house in the Marina.

"I can't help you," he said.

When I could talk, I said, "What happened to the guy who vanished?"

"Still gone," he said. "That was his wife on the phone."

"You're talking to this guy's wife with that sexy voice?"

I think they learn it in law school, that dead look. It's almost as good as a cop's. Then he gave me one-tenth of a smile, confiding, wanting to be friendly.

I could see it: With me out of here, his life would be so much simpler.

At the age of eight, I wanted to be a ballerina. They were those creatures on television, the ones drifting across the stage, women so beautiful nothing could hurt them.

My parents took me to a few ballets at the Opera House in San Francisco. They looked on politely, clapping when it was time to applaud, but I think they looked forward to the intermissions, the white wine, the chance to see friends.

Ballet lessons were not at all what I had imagined. There were too many tarnished mirrors floor to ceiling, too many other students. The woman who taught the classes was one of those beautiful swans. I think she stayed thin by not wasting time being nice to students. *Glide, Maureen—glide, not stumble.*

I felt for the ceramic frog in the ballet slipper. Maybe I was hoping it had vanished on its own.

I could hear my father's voice downstairs, on the phone. I could hear him laugh affectionately.

In Canada now, in the far north, my mother and Adler were together. Maybe it would be a cold night, the stars everywhere, reflected in the lake. Mother and Adler close together, huddling for warmth.

··· 18 ···

The days passed.

I watched myself in shop windows, my image rippling along, changing shape.

I felt giddy, fluttery. Maybe I would sneak the frog back into Maureen's house. After two or three days, giving it back would have been like giving Maureen and her family a gift, offering a present to all of them.

It would be a confession, even if they didn't see me slipping it back into place. But the frog wasn't the problem. The problem was: What little surprise would I pull next?

Besides, if I forgot about it, it wasn't there.

I kept busy, dropping by the Berkeley Municipal Court to watch a trial or two. A woman had been arrested for soliciting. She perched there prim and calm, next to her cool, gray-haired woman lawyer. The assistant district attorney fingered his pen and talked about the laws against prostitution, how a community has standards, how these standards go back to the beginning of what we call morality.

Night after night I didn't sleep so much as lie there. I got blue circles under my eyes, and the color drained from my face. I didn't look that bad, if you like dead bodies.

Over the days I spent a lot of time with Maureen.

Sometimes she couldn't talk much, depressed because of a news story. Hordes of emus in western

Australia killed themselves running into an electric fence. In France twenty cows were burned alive when lightning struck the barn where they had drawn together for safety. To Maureen these misfortunes were evidence of the callousness of human beings. We could go on about our lives while things like this happened.

Sometimes she was gleeful over something she had just taught Lincoln to do. He fetched the chewed-up tennis ball out of the closet when she said "ball." He snouted the mail out of the mailbox when she gave the order, if the mail carrier was far enough away from the house.

She and her father and her mother did not seem to notice what was gone.

It was a freedom I didn't want.

We were in the backyard, in the big bare place Lincoln had worn in the grass. It was late in the afternoon, shadows, a chill in the air. My caramel purse was leaning against a tree, not far from Lincoln's plastic water dish. Mother and Adler would be back from their trip tomorrow.

The Frisbee had a crack in it, and it glided badly, rolling along the ground. All the tennis balls were chewed to yellow-green bits. I felt the homey pleasure of Maureen's family, leaving each other notes reminding each other to water the coffee plant.

I was trying to get Lincoln to give me a fragment of red rubber ball. He wouldn't let me have it.

"Give," commanded Maureen. She was wearing a huge blue T-shirt that showed her bra straps. There was a faded image on the shirt, a University of California Golden Bear.

Lincoln wouldn't let her have it, either.

I couldn't stop myself. I heard myself say, "Maureen, I did something I shouldn't have done."

A part of me wanted to stop and hit rewind, but it was too late.

Sometimes she can look so stupid. "Like what?"

I was very fifties, capris and a polka-dot blouse and teeny Italian sandals. The brand-new sole was so thin I could feel every pebble, every leaf, underfoot.

"Take a look in my purse." I had hoped to toss this out in an offhand way, but I didn't think I managed to sound very confident.

She stopped looking at me, turning to Lincoln, holding out her hand for the ball.

I let a moment pass. I wondered if I could just shut up and let the subject die. Maybe Maureen wasn't even listening, thinking about something she'd heard on the news, listening to music in her head.

I heard myself say, "I think you'll be surprised."

I was wasting my time. She wasn't paying much attention, yanking the chewed-up ball out of Lincoln's teeth. The ball looked like raw hamburger.

Okay, I told myself, I'll forget about it. Case closed. It was almost a relief. I confessed and no one heard, no one cared.

Her glance was a question. She wasn't in the mood for me today.

I gave her a little unsteady smile. She would have to see for herself.

She picked up the purse.

"Open it," I said.

She worked the snap, one knee on her jeans torn, a pair of rubber sandals on her feet, one toenail with just a trace of red polish.

It was in her hand, a bundle of tissue paper held together with Scotch tape, neatly. Maureen sniffed the scented paper, and gave me a look.

"Are you okay?" she asked without much interest.

"Open it," I said.

"What are you doing?" she asked, vaguely impatient with me, like all this was an interruption she could do without.

I waited.

She tore the tissue paper, and tore it again until she could see what was there, nestled in her hand.

I didn't say the words. I just let her figure it out.

It took her a moment, but she got the point.

At last she said, "It's no wonder."

Okay, I told myself. It was over. But I stayed where I was.

"I know how your mind works," Maureen said. "You don't think there's anyone else. You see us talking, moving around, but it doesn't really touch you." She didn't say this like someone delivering criticism. She sounded frank, dead calm.

I could leave now.

"Wait." Maureen gave Lincoln the Frisbee, and he threw it into the air himself, and caught it. "You have to explain something."

There was a rattle and a creak from behind me. Her

father came through the side gate, wheeling his decrepit bicycle. "I think—heh—the university wants to get rid of me," he said.

Maureen and I must have just stared at him. I was glad for a break in the action, but at the same time I wished he wasn't there.

She kept the frog wrapped in the white paper. He couldn't see what it was. He looked at Maureen and he looked at me, and must have realized he was interrupting. He went on, "The chairman bought me a turkey sandwich—heh—and all he talked about was early retirement."

I wanted to tell this kind man what I had done. I wanted to tell him that I had never wanted to hurt him.

"Red polka dots," said Mr. Dean, smiling at me. "I used to have a tie like that. I wore it on my twenty-first birthday." Then he gave a little nod, an apology for interrupting, and leaned the bike against the back porch.

When her father was inside, I took Maureen's arm. She pulled herself away. I knew: It would be different between us from now on.

"Do you think people are happy to see you, Anna? Do you think people are *hey, Anna's coming, she's always so much fun?*"

All this in a tight, quiet voice. I kept quiet.

"Everything you do is—*everybody, look at me.* You don't have any right to hurt my family."

I was at the gate when she said, "Don't come over here anymore."

She didn't say this like someone who was angry. She said this like someone who saw the truth, sure she was right. But I could see something else in her eyes: She wanted me to say something. This was one fight she didn't really want to win.

I managed a smile. She didn't have to worry. I was never coming back.

··· 19 ···

The pool van was there, right behind the Mustang.

I was surprised at how much I did not want to see Barry. Even from my bedroom I could hear the whine of the Pool Vac, residue being sucked off the bottom of the pool. Dad paid extra for him to come twice a week and fine-tune the chlorine.

I sprinkled some fish food into the tank, leaving the cap off the container so Dad wouldn't feed them later that evening. You feed them too much, something bad happens, gill rot, or you have to buy those snails that eat green scum off the inside of the tank.

I didn't know what Mother had planned. Maybe I was going to pick out my own bedroom furniture. I was going to sit with a big book of wallpaper in my lap while she and Adler looked over my shoulder.

No, Adler would say, she doesn't want that little

flower pattern wallpaper. He would close the book. Anna doesn't want an antique walnut dresser, Adler would say. She doesn't want a big pink bowl of cloves and crushed rose petals to make her room smell nice.

Adler would be right.

I put on a sandwashed silk sundress, sleeveless, with a button front. I wore shoes I had found under a sign that read FLATTERY FOR YOUR FOOT, navy blue slip-on espadrilles, imported, handmade, not cheap.

The purse I tugged off the shelf in the closet was a tight-weave straw classic, wide-bottomed, with coiled straps. I had money—a little—aspirin, Tums, cigarettes.

I put some panties and some roll-on deodorant into a gym bag. I made myself not look back at the house. I got into the car, started it up, and rolled down to the end of the street.

A dog ran from the sidewalk, bounding in front of the car. My foot was slow, my reaction time terrible, reflexes rusty.

I found the brake pedal and the wheels locked. The car slid briefly, and then came to a rocking stop.

"Lincoln!" I shoved against the door until it opened.

I stood in the street. Lincoln was unhurt, gazing at me with mild, friendly curiosity. His mouth was open, tongue hanging. He was trailing his long length of gray rope.

"Lincoln, get in the car," I said.

He obeyed at once, not even hesitating. He even knew where to sit, the passenger's side, eager to go for a ride.

··· 20 ···

It was early evening, the traffic jam a mess of brake lights.

The radio didn't work very well, a connection loose, Dad had said, between the antenna and the dash. I could barely pick up KGO, trying to find out if this was all the way to Hayward or just through Oakland. A dump truck had spilled some gravel out across all the lanes, and everyone slowed down to go over the little blue rocks.

Lincoln put his nose against the window on his side, smearing it with dog sweat.

Then I was past the gravel, and I headed east, past Castro Valley, feeling that little bit of excitement and happiness that going somewhere gives.

Sometimes I hate cars. You sit there in a box, looking at the scenery through glass. A car is like television, hour after hour on the same channel, except you can run into something and get killed.

I'm not that experienced at driving on freeways. The car floats. You think you'll be aiming the car between the lines and the car will roll straight. But it doesn't, the car floats one way or another. I had to make minor adjustments, moving the steering wheel a little bit this way, a little bit that way.

I was having imaginary conversations. I have a Porta-Mom in my head, and when I get bored or tired I have my own talk show: Anna Teresa Charles and her guest visitor, the same one she has every night.

You know a lot about yourself, but nothing about life, said the Mom-voice. *You mean I don't know what it's like to work in an office with no windows,* I said back. *You mean I don't know what it's like to sit in a meeting and tell the weatherman what kind of neckties he ought to wear.*

I could imagine her eyes bright, the shake of her head, her sad, bitter *You're so sure of yourself.*

I never get bored with this kind of talk in my head, even though it's tedious and painful. It just plays on and on, a radio that won't turn off.

Lincoln put his nose at the top of the window, savoring the traffic smells, and then the farms and orchards. I couldn't see the land, but we both knew it was out there. I had traveled to Disneyland with my parents years before, and this was how we went, down Highway 5, past the farmland and the foothills, cattle, orchards, but most of all vacant land with nothing much on it.

The Mustang held steady, a little vibration in the steering wheel, what Mr. Friedlander, the auto shop teacher, would have diagnosed as bad front-end alignment. I don't usually drive fast, though, fifty-five is all right. I didn't like the way the car started to shake even worse when I passed a few trucks.

After a while the chatter from the Inner Mom shut up and I didn't let myself think. A few nights of bad sleep had left me empty. The radio reception continued to be trouble. I expected to hear country western music but it was news, when I got anything at all, the stock exchange and floods somewhere in Georgia.

I felt self-conscious pulling into a Chevron station. It

was ridiculous to think this way, but I did. Everyone would look at me and see how far I was from Capistrano Street, in a car I had never driven past Hilltop Mall. There was a *self* island and a *full* island and I drove in beside *self*. I pumped super unleaded. I felt a little clumsy, but only a little. I took my time scrubbing dead bugs off the windshield, wings, thoraxes, all kinds of insect parts.

There was heat coming out of the radiator. That's what radiators do, they remove the high temperature from the engine and release it into the air. I could explain this to the least capable student in the class, Harry Luke, a guy who came to school to eat lunch with his girlfriend, and who saw classes as a way to fill in the time before and after.

Lincoln peed on a tumbleweed at the edge of the lighted area, and I let him drink some water straight from the pink hose, getting water on my sundress. I wondered if I should take the cap off the radiator and pour in some more coolant. Mr. Friedlander had warned that taking the radiator cap off a hot car could be dangerous, a geyser exploding as soon as the cap was loose. I left the radiator alone.

I checked the oil, wiping the dipstick and reinserting it, careful to keep the black syrup away from my dress. The oil was down about a quart, so I bought some forty-weight oil and emptied it into the oil intake, and felt satisfied that I had taken care of things.

There would be plenty of time to call Dad and let him know I was all right. I paid a man in a booth and asked if there were any maps.

A vending machine sold maps, and it took only quarters, so I had to go back and ask the man in the glass booth to break a five. I felt awkward, sure he would say that they didn't give change, the way some stores will if you need to make a phone call.

I tossed the map into the backseat after a glance. I steered the car up the on-ramp back onto the freeway. I was worried about the oil, and, now that I was back on the freeway, having to pass a slow truck, I was worried about the other fluids I hadn't checked, and for the first time I really doubted what I was doing.

This wasn't a doubt that originated in the voice of my imaginary mother. This originated in me. I was already two hundred miles south and I was afraid the car wasn't going to be able to make the trip as far as I wanted to go, not in this heat. The sun was gone, but with the window rolled down I could feel the warm wind. Moths flattened on the windshield, tattered flags that the wind loosened and blew away.

I turned on the radio again, and even the static sounded calming, sputters that meant there was activity out there in the world, even though I couldn't make out what it was.

When I told Lincoln we were doing fine he gave me one of those dog laughs, eyes blinking, mouth wide.

Maureen thought she understood animals better than anyone else, but I don't think she took such good care of Lincoln. I even let Lincoln lick my hand a little. He was polite, his tongue hot, but he was more interested in the smells flowing in through the barely open window.

When I said something to him he would look, wag, and put his snout back to the window. Sometimes the vibration in the steering was so bad I hung on hard, but after a while, I got used to it, driving like a person who did this all the time.

··· 21 ···

Interstate 5 intersects with Interstate 10. You look at the map and you think it looks complicated, but I told myself that in real life all you have to do is pay attention.

It was past midnight. The LA traffic was heavy, cars driving up behind me, all headlights and speed, almost touching my bumper. I hung on hard to the steering wheel, telling myself to stay calm.

I watched for the sign, and took the turnoff. If you want to go to Covina or La Verne, this is the road to take. I passed by what I knew must be towns of strip malls and gas stations, with the occasional condo complex thrown in for variety. My hands were sweating.

I took 15 north, feeling the risk I was taking. If I missed a turnoff, I'd drive forever through places where criminals waited for strangers to get out and ask directions. Lincoln slept in the small backseat. The seat was just about big enough for him, and now and then he took a long, deep breath in his sleep and let it out with a comfortable groan.

I had the directions memorized from an old post-card, a half-joking challenge: *Hey, if you don't have anything better to do come out and see me.*

It was harder than I had thought to keep it all in mind, Foothill Avenue, Colton Avenue, all the way over a long series of hills in the road. I remember he told me once he took them at about eighty in a Honda Accord one night and the little car never once leaped off the road, life not like the movies.

I turned left at Arroyo Avenue, thinking how foolish I was, like someone marching in to take a test cold, not even five minutes studying, and thinking: None of these questions make any sense.

I thought he lived in the desert.

This was a lost, dead town, vacant lots, stucco walls, dark except for streetlights. There was a mountain up ahead, at the end of the road, a canyon opening up, a jumble of white boulders in the bad light.

Along the street were squat, ordinary houses, plastic tricycles and skateboards on the gravel where in normal places a front lawn would be. Some houses had a car parked right up in front of the house, under the picture window, and two or three cars jammed into the driveway.

The mailbox was one of the usual silvery aluminum boxes, with the numbers written neatly in Magic Marker, 22219. I couldn't see the house very well, but I sensed another one-story stucco box behind a spiky, cactus-type plant.

Lincoln was awake now, sniffing my ear. He scrambled over the bucket seat and put his nose to the window crack.

I turned off the engine. Everything was quiet. I had lost track of the time, but I had to guess it was one in the morning, or even later. The numbers on the mailbox were drawn in what looked like a familiar way, carefully, by someone who could get a job painting signs if he had to.

I sat in the car. The pea gravel in the front lawn was pale, and there were old thrown-away newspapers on the walkway up to the house. It had to be a mistake.

I told Lincoln I would be back. He whined and made one of his half barks, half words, but he stayed put.

I would either have the right house and everything would be wonderful or I would have the wrong house and it would be embarrassing, but nothing worse than that. I got out of the car, bringing my purse, and holding the car keys in my hand, like they were proof of my harmless intentions.

The car made cooling, metallic ticks sitting there, giving off heat as I passed it. My feet crunched the white gravel that had crept up over the walkway to the front steps, and every detail about the place was wrong.

It's not a good feeling, standing in a place thinking: wrong street, wrong town. There was a far-off television sound, laughter, a voice. Even the doorbell was wrong, a black button encircled by a tarnished yellow metal. I gave the button a push.

Someone was there sooner than I expected, so suddenly I stepped back and put a hand to my throat.

A large figure stood behind the screen door, a silhouette in front of the glow of living-room light. There was a long moment when nothing moved. The screen door opened with a dry little creak.

But still nothing was happening, nothing human, nothing that mattered.

Arms opened and took me in.

It was like winning the contest, numbers flashing, applause. Say hello to America, Anna Teresa.

That's what he was calling me, with a big hug, my feet off the ground. "Anna Teresa!"

Only Ted calls me that, my first two names. And only Ted gives those big, breath-squeezing hugs. But I was speechless, looking up at Ted when we were inside, a man as tall as Dad and looking like him, too.

"You look different," Ted was saying.

"Worse," I suggested.

"Dad was worried sick. He had an idea you were heading my way," said Ted.

"I drove down," I said, realizing as I said it how dumb I sounded, saying something unnecessary.

"Any trouble?" People always say this, meaning: How was your trip, meaning: It's good to see you.

"I need your help, Ted," I said, near tears.

"I bet you're hungry," he said.

"I have to talk to you," I said, barely getting the words out. But I began to feel a sense of security. I was okay now. Nothing bad could happen to me here.

Ted was brisk, businesslike, very friendly but also very much in charge. He called up Dad and handed me the phone, and I told Dad I was here and that the car had driven perfectly well, no problems. I told him I was sorry I hadn't left a note, but it was all right now.

Dad just kept saying, "God, Anna, if you had only just said something—"

I told him he was right, but he wasn't.

When I was off the phone, I went into the bathroom and peed and after that I took a look at myself in the mirror over the sink. I looked like a drawing in a coloring book, places where eyes and lips would be when you color them in.

··· 22 ···

A voice in my head said: You forgot.

I ran out of the house, car keys in my hand.

Lincoln jumped up on Ted. Ted half-patted, half-wrestled the dog down with a laugh. "Lincoln, you have no manners." I sighed. I had further proof that the Deans did not know how to deal with a dog.

"Why don't you buy him a leash?" Ted worked at the knot at Lincoln's collar and tossed the gray rope into a corner.

"That's a good idea," I said.

Ted cranked open a can of Bonnie Hubbard beef hash. Lincoln wolfed it in thirty seconds. Then he left the room and I could hear sloppy, lapping noises, Lincoln drinking out of the toilet.

"How long have you had a dog?" asked Ted.

"Not long," I said.

I sat at a small kitchen table with a toaster and a stack of paper napkins still in the package, the top torn open so you could pull out a napkin when you needed one. There was a peanut-butter jar that held pencils, yellow eraser-tipped pencils and the blue pencils for drafting.

Lincoln made his way in, the nails of his paws making clicking noises on the tiles. He lay down against a wall. Ted was stirring some tomato soup at a stove, an old range with black knobs. He poured the soup into a bowl and crumbled saltines into it without asking, the way we always liked it as children. I hadn't eaten tomato soup like that since seventh grade, but I didn't say anything.

Ted was making a big show of pouring me milk and offering me some Pepperidge Farm chocolate chip cookies, but he was chattering. Ted had never talked like this, filler talk, stuff you say when you are getting used to having a visitor. I had expected to sit down with Ted and start with the important subjects.

Ted was telling me he knew I could read a map. He hadn't left the porch light on because it was broken. The landlord was a man who lived in Hemet; all Ted had to do was send the rent check to a PO box. Ted said he was usually asleep by now, but he had stayed up, expecting me.

Chatter. It was good to see him and hear him, but Ted was different now. He was tanned, and his hair was the same color as Dad's, dirty blond. I had the feeling Ted might have gotten a tattoo or something, made some drastic alteration in himself. But I looked him up and down, Levi's and a white V-necked T-shirt, and running shoes with no laces, the feet just stuck in, slipper-fashion. He needed a shave.

"I had to talk to you," I said.

"You're having trouble," he said, sitting down across from me.

He was sipping a glass of milk, nonfat, the only kind either of us would drink. He was sitting looking at me, patient and friendly. This was the Ted I wanted.

"So much has been happening," I began. And then I couldn't talk, looking around at the yellow, speckled floor. I had so much to say I couldn't say anything.

"The sofa's pretty comfortable," he said. "I set out some blankets."

I shook my head. How could I even think of sleep?

"We have time," he said. "All kinds of time."

I blinked, clearing my vision. I found myself considering his words. *All kinds of time.* I couldn't finish my soup.

"Look how tired you are," he said. "You drove five hundred miles today."

I couldn't help being irritated with Ted. I was with him at last and he was saying the same kind of thing Dad says, trying to be nice and giving me a caring, interested look, but about two chapters behind.

"Mother wants me to move in with her," I said.

"Well, I can understand that being a problem," Ted

said. He was in an orbit far from Mom and Dad, and when he couldn't make it to Mom's wedding, no one was really surprised.

"She's not the person she used to be," I said. I had almost said *the same wretch she used to be*.

"Years of therapy, working at last," he said.

"She's trying to be reasonable, the poor thing," I said. I meant to roll my eyes when I said this, but my timing was off, and the statement came out flat, truthful.

He smiled, but there was something wrong with him.

"You're tired," I said.

"I have to get up in the morning," he said.

I hesitated. The saltines collect at the bottom of the bowl. I stirred the floury paste for a moment. "You haven't met Adler," I said.

"What's he like?"

Sometimes a question is too big.

I was tired after all. Tired and used up. The kitchen was small, dishes in a rack, a coffee mug, a glass. I had half-expected my brother to be living with someone. There was a shelf, salt and pepper, instant coffee, Hershey's powdered cocoa. My brother and I are crazy about the stuff.

"Connie moved out," he said.

Reading my mind. It's nice to have a brother, but a little scary, as though he might know something about me that I had forgotten.

It was early, the room gray light.

Lincoln's snout was in my face. The furniture was sagging, tattered at the corners, including the sofa I was lying on. One of the seat cushions had fallen off the sofa during the night.

I was crippled. I hunched over to the TV and turned it on. I kept the sound off, the way Dad does, looking at the screen to make sure life is still going on. I heard Ted in the bedroom, a drawer opening and closing. I was about to beat him to the bathroom, something I used to be pretty good at, but he got there first.

There was a collection of things on the coffee table, cigarettes, my purse, a *Scientific American*. The pages were stuck together with what looked like spilled Coke. My espadrilles toed together on the carpet. My dress was on the floor. I like silk, but it tends to wrinkle. The woman at Maxi's says I may be more of a cotton person.

Lincoln whined at the back door and I let him out. There was a concrete patio with a barbecue. Lincoln squatted beside a hibiscus with three blossoms.

When Ted was out of the bathroom and thumping around in the bedroom, I moved fast. My brother has nice soap, Neutrogena, soothing, with a clean smell. I took a shower and washed my hair with his yucca blossom shampoo.

I wandered into the kitchen, drying my hair with a Gold's Gym towel. Ted was making cocoa for two, using real sugar. When he took the cocoa out of the microwave, it was delicious.

Lincoln was back in the kitchen, nosing the air.

"A dog like that must eat a lot," said Ted.

"I thought you were something big in landscaping," I said.

"We have to hurry," Ted replied. "I'm running late."

He was shaved and smelled of aftershave, his hair combed back. He was twenty-three, and had been in and out of college, UCLA, Fullerton State. He wore a denim shirt with an orange undershirt showing at the collar, and the same Levi's as the night before. He was wearing work shoes, scuffed and old, with new red laces.

I should have expected this, but it surprised me. Despite what he had said the night before, I had imagined him taking the day off.

"You landscape the yard here?" I said.

He put toast into the toaster, an ancient appliance with blackened crumbs all over the top.

"Those old newspapers out on the front step," I continued. "I like that casual, sun-baked look. Nice touch.

"Beautiful job on the backyard, too," I said.

He didn't respond. He kept smiling, starting to hum something under his breath.

"Good cocoa," I said.

He said, "You don't have to drink it."

I was going to be quiet for a while, eat toast and plum jam, look out the window at the smog between the back door and the mountains. But I found myself saying, "I thought you would live someplace nice."

"You're disappointed," he said.

"Someplace Zen, raked sand and a few maple trees, maybe a pool, a few fish."

"Maybe a monk," he said, "propped against a rock."

"All I see is cement."

He opened a can of Spam and put it on a plate by the back door. The dog nosed it around the floor, having trouble picking it up. Ted put a slice of toast on a plate and gave it to me. He let his piece cool for a while in the toaster and then picked it out and ate it, no butter, no jam.

I shut up. Maybe he was in a bad mood. He would start quoting things like, "That which does not kill me makes me strong," or the one about it's easier to get a camel through the eye of a needle than to get into heaven if you have any kind of taste in clothes.

"The sofa was pretty comfortable," I said.

"I'm saving up for some new things," he said. "A new sofa, a television, maybe a home entertainment center." He said this ironically, but he probably had something expensive planned, something that would make Beethoven echo off the canyons.

I said, "I see how you can use some entertainment."

We left Lincoln tied to a water pipe in the concrete emptiness of the backyard. We left him with a plastic basin full of water. Ted tied a triple knot in the gray rope, but I was sure Lincoln would get it undone and escape. There was nothing I could do.

Ted drove a red Toyota pickup. The *Toyota* on the tailgate had been partly colored in to read *OYO*

His neighborhood was even worse in daylight,

chain-link fences and pregnant women with five little children. We drove through housing tracts, some new, some worn-out, until we got to some open space.

"Connie and I didn't exactly break up," he said, responding to my question. "She decided she didn't like living with me. It was a setback, but I'll see her Friday night."

Lincoln was going to be gone when I got back. I looked out at the ash-gray scenery, hating it.

"We're clearing boulders," said Ted, driving fast, much faster than I usually go. "Tearing out some sage, some creosote. We used to have a bigger crew, but one guy popped a nerve in his neck and another guy had something wrong with his green card. Immigration people arrested him. And one guy got bit by a baby rattlesnake. He couldn't handle the stress. So the rest of us are busy."

"You talk like this all the time now?" I asked.

He looked over at me, his glance saying: Like what?

"You used to talk like a book, Thoreau or someone. Now you sound like a work jock."

"We have a break at ten-thirty," he said, after a very long pause.

The contractor was a tall man with a beer belly and a cowboy hat. He was called Wade and he swore a lot. He said the immigration people were a bunch of jerk-offs. He said anyone who got bit by a baby rattlesnake had their heads so far up their butts you could just roll them along the ground.

But he said I could sit in the cab of his pickup, where

it was air-conditioned, and he didn't say it with a look, the way some men do, meaning: Spend some time next to me and I'll show you a couple of moves.

Wade just ignored me in a friendly way, and I sat and watched Ted drive a down-size Deere tractor, dragging a dry field flat. There were papers on the front seat beside me, manila folders and legal documents, an environmental-impact report, and a letter to a company that was late with a shipment of crushed granite.

These forms were interesting, county and state commissions having to be satisfied that no pollutants were going to drain from the new golf course into the water table. There was a letter to the immigration department about harassing skilled employees on-site. I spotted a couple of typos.

Wade opened the door and used the phone on the dash to make a phone call, hanging up when there was no answer.

"You ought to get one of those computer programs that check spelling," I said.

He looked at me from under his cowboy hat.

"I just thought I'd mention it," I said.

··24··

At ten-thirty a snack truck pulled up. It was a white pickup with aluminum doors that opened to display plastic containers of flavored yogurt and several kinds of donuts, including plain, glazed, and chocolate-covered, and cinnamon rolls in cellophane.

At lunch another truck swung into the parking lot, and we ate burritos and prepackaged sandwiches. I ate a ham sandwich on white bread with dill pickles that soaked through the bread and made it soggy and green. I had a diet 7-Up. The drinks were in a bed of ice. When you picked one out it left a can-shaped cavity. The woman in charge put another can into the hollow to get cold.

All day I sat there, getting the point. This was how Ted lived, working under a smoggy sky.

I lounged in the truck and listened to the radio, which could be adjusted so you got police calls. The dispatcher was a woman with one of those bone-numb, bored voices. There was a man on Baseline Road the dispatcher said was fifty-one fifty. I knew that meant mentally disturbed. The man was naked, running from backyard to backyard, swinging over fences. The police apprehended him, and after he was in custody the police calls weren't very interesting.

At last shadows fell from the mountains, softening the outline of the rocks and the clawed hill. It was still hot, and there was a smell of skunk in the air.

Ted was dusty, his boots and his pants white with it. He was sweating and his hair stood up all around his head. "Have a good day?" he asked.

I didn't want to tell him how I felt.

We drove to a restaurant called La Estrellita, a pink stucco place only a few blocks from where Ted lived. "You aren't going to go home and take a shower?" I asked.

Music was playing, a song I could tell was sad, a town the man would never see, a place more beautiful than any town he had ever known. I could make out most of the Spanish, and what I couldn't I understood anyway. I thought that surely Ted couldn't sit in here all dusty and sweaty like that, but people at other tables looked tired and dusty, too.

We ate gigantic tacos, tacos piled with refritos and avocado and sour cream. I drank iced tea and Ted had a Dos Equis.

"I wouldn't attract the attention of the immigration people," I said. It was good to let him know I could handle a job in construction if I wanted to.

Ted swallowed, dabbed his mouth with a napkin with the name of the restaurant on it in red. He looked like he didn't want to talk about immigration troubles. His face was thinner than I remembered it, and he hadn't shaved very well, a little patch of whiskers under his nose. "Wade knows what he's doing."

"Maybe he hires someone working on someone else's Social Security number," I said. "Maybe Wade knows when he hires the person, maybe Wade doesn't.

If Wade complains too much about the border people, they might start investigating more carefully. Maybe Wade should just forget about the guy with the green card problem."

"That's a good point," said Ted.

His halfhearted compliment made me feel self-conscious. "I was just thinking."

"The legal mind," he said.

"I want to live with you," I said. It came out suddenly, and there it was, something I hadn't even been aware of thinking. "I don't mean just the summer. I mean, move here, finish my senior year. I could get a job, maybe work for Wade in an office."

Ted gave it some thought. "You like my house?"

I chewed a piece of tortilla.

"My backyard?" asked Ted. He looked ridiculous with his hair like that, all messed up, like someone who tried to look insane on purpose. "You like the patio with no sign of life but one hibiscus?"

"You have nice soap in the shower," I said.

"I don't want you living with me," Ted said. He didn't say it like someone being cruel. He said it in a kind tone, but it was like a slap. "You can stay the summer, and I'll be glad to have you. But you can't run away from your problems."

I let three beats pass before I said anything. The family counselor at Kaiser suggested this once as a way of not saying hurtful things. "You'll never graduate from college," I said. "All your plans add up to eating glue sandwiches for lunch beside a golf course for retired people."

"So you couldn't stand living with me anyway," he said, as though he had just proved something.

"I don't want your help, Ted," I said. There were tears in my eyes but my voice was steady. "You're right. I see how you're going to live the rest of your life and I don't want to sit around on your flea-market furniture."

"You can talk to Mother," said Ted. "Or Dad. Try it. Don't be such a coward."

I was out of the booth, straightening the wrinkles in my dress.

It was just about dark. The parking lot was filling up. A big shiny pickup truck crammed with men in baseball caps slowed down and took a look at me.

I didn't care. I let them look. One of them said something, and the rest of them laughed. The truck rolled away, gravel *snap crackle pop* under the oversize tires.

Ted called to me.

"Where are you going?" he said when he caught up.

"Walking to your place," I said.

"You won't be able to find it," he said.

"I'll find it."

"You won't be able to get in," he said. "I keep it locked. I bought window stoppers at one of those security stores. The windows won't slide open."

I didn't bother telling him that if I wanted to get in, I would.

I was afraid of what I was going to do, but I didn't have any choice.

···25···

Ted and I didn't really have much to say for a while.

I had already made up my mind. I was uneasy when I thought about what I had to do, but I was realistic. I made myself stop thinking.

We drove the few blocks through the darkness, and when we got there, Lincoln was standing in the front yard, bounding around like he was too happy to stay on the ground, he wanted to practice flying.

I held the dog by his collar and took him through the house to the back and tied him up again. He kept wanting to jump up and down. I tied a monster knot, one I invented on the spot, and tugged it hard, Lincoln licking my ear. I turned on the spigot at the side of the house and filled up his plastic basin.

Ted wrestled the top off a can of chicken meat and put it in a bowl with some leftover macaroni and cheese. When he took it outside, Lincoln gobbled the food, and when it was gone, he licked the concrete around the plate.

"What does he usually eat?" Ted asked.

"Dog food," I said.

Ted said he felt like watching television. He said there was rum raisin ice cream in the fridge. He wasn't sulking, or acting clipped and cold the way Mother did after a fight. He acted like he wanted to avoid me for awhile, maybe hoping I'd get over my mood. He fingered the remote and watched a show with the sound off, penguins standing around.

I had a glass of water. It tasted like dirt. I went outside and watched the lights of airplanes drift across the stars. Lincoln's rope wasn't long enough for him to come and sit beside me. He came as far as he could and lay on his belly. He whined a little, a quiet whistling noise.

I listened while Ted made a phone call. I tensed up, but he was talking about what dumb videos they had at the mall. I could tell by the way he used his voice, sounding confident and caring, that he must be talking to Connie.

When he was off the phone, he came out beside me on the patio. "Hear that?" he said.

Hear what? I wanted to ask. I assumed he was referring to how cool he sounded on the telephone just then, showing off, something he rarely did. Maybe Connie had agreed to leave for Las Vegas tonight, a package marriage—rings, chapel, and deluxe suite— and he was breaking the news.

I knew that Adler and Mother must be back now. They would be unpacking, or maybe they would leave that for tomorrow, go right to bed.

"Coyotes," said Ted.

There had been a puppylike yammering in the distance, not a sound to catch my attention compared with the faint rumble of jets and the muttering of various televisions in the neighborhood.

Lincoln was standing still, nose toward the sound.

"They sound like little dogs," I said.

"They aren't little," he said. "They aren't dogs."

Ted liked sounding this way, knowledgeable, tough.

I realized how little I knew. I tucked my feet under the chair I was in, a folding aluminum chair with little corrosion bubbles on the arms. Rattlesnakes, I thought. Scorpions.

I felt his touch in my hair. I don't like to be touched there. It just messes it up, even though I keep it casual, wash and wear. The sun around here would color it, not to mention fry it dry. "I didn't bring enough clothes," I said.

"You don't make a lot of sense sometimes," said Ted.

I had forgotten my cigarettes again, left them in the living room. Maybe I wasn't a cigarette smoker anymore. It happens: You aren't what you used to be.

The phone rang in the kitchen. Ted had one of those houses where everything was out of date, the telephone fastened to the wall, the refrigerator with a plastic ice tray you had to bend in your hands to loosen the cubes.

Ted didn't move, looking down at me.

I made a gesture—go ahead and answer it.

I think we both knew who it was before he even approached the kitchen. I could hear him inside, the way he said, "Hello, Mom," a little loudly so I could hear.

Yes, I heard him say. She's here. There was a longer pause, and I knew what kind of questions she was asking.

Instead of answering questions, though, Ted was just saying, "Yes. Sure," listening, making encouraging sounds. "That's right."

If you didn't know Ted, you'd think he sounded casual, easygoing, an ordinary guy talking to his mom, no problem. I could hear it, though, the tension resurrecting itself. Mother had fought with each of us, swearing that we would send her to a mental hospital.

I have to wonder sometimes what animals are trying to say, they spend so much time making noise.

"I don't think she wants to talk," said Ted. "She's out on the patio, looking at the stars."

I could imagine what my mother pictured. She imagined a luxuriant patio with broad-leafed plants, a little fountain trickling in the corner, ferns. Adler was probably in the same room with her, his hands folded, waiting patiently for her to get off the phone.

"I won't," Ted was saying. "Don't worry," he said with a tired chuckle.

The coyotes were there, yammering like puppies in pain.

···26···

A couple of crickets started up, over by the hibiscus. Ted stayed on the phone for a while, and I gazed up at the sky.

The stars were an invisible net stretched tight by tiny silver pins. I can feel the net attached to my own private darkness, my secret sky.

Maureen would know what I was talking about, but she would be distracted by things that didn't bother me. She would hear the clatter of a trash can lid several houses away and say she bet nobody recycled cans around here, just threw them away.

He was off the phone, there beside me on the patio, hands in his pockets, his shadow, in the light from the kitchen, falling all the way to the fence.

"She's worried," he said. "She wants you to call her."

I didn't bother to respond.

"You should," he said.

"What were you saying?" I asked.

"Mom told me not to let you drive me crazy," he said.

How nice of her, I thought, to show such interest in both of us. "She'd be shocked," I said, "if she knew you couldn't afford new work boots."

He looked down at his feet. "These are just getting broken in, Anna."

No more Anna Teresa. No more brotherly calm. He was impatient, weary. "I pay my own rent," he said. "I buy my groceries. I'm learning how to lay sprinklers."

"That's an amazing branch of science," I said. "Sprinklers."

He shook his head, took a deep breath and let it out. I could sense him full of things he wanted to say.

"Maybe Wade'll start you in on weed pulling," I said. "Let you study that for a few years."

"You can't get far in Southern California landscaping without a feel for irrigation," he said.

"The drip system," I said. "Tubes leading right to the base of each little plant."

"It's efficient," he said.

I looked around at the blank concrete for a moment, knowing his eyes were on me. "I counted on you. I thought you were special, Ted. I thought you, of all people, could really do something wonderful with your life."

I couldn't stop myself.

I wanted to tell him I was sorry, that I didn't mean what I was saying, but he was walking back toward the house, a figure like my father, too much on his mind.

I got up out of the chair, and the frame was trapped around my leg, dragging along with me until I shook myself free. He was already inside, back in the living room, probably, sitting on the sofa. I bit my knuckle until it hurt.

I knew what I had to do. If I stayed here, I would keep after him, sting him like this again and again. There was nothing I could do about it. I would turn into a cartoon version of myself, like the Aquascan man, a little body and a big mouth that wouldn't shut up. I would cripple his life. There was only one favor I could do him, and I knew what it was.

·· 27 ··

I told him that I appreciated all his help. He turned and looked at me, his hand on the light switch. His look was hopeful, skeptical, half giving up on me. "Anything I can do," he said.

When people say things like this, they don't mean it. What they mean is that they care what happens to you, that you aren't alone.

We were being very careful not to start a conversation with any feeling in it. I wore one of his shirts, a T-shirt several sizes too big, a washed-out pool-bottom blue. He was pink and tousled from a hot shower, and he looked drained, too tired to stand there talking.

Lincoln had whined so much Ted had let him in. Now the dog was wedged between the easy chair and the coffee table, half asleep. When he took a deep breath the table shifted a little.

"You haven't really changed," I said. "You're still Ted, inside."

He smiled, lifted one shoulder, let it fall: maybe.

"Mother's still the same, too," I said. "Inside she still can't stand either one of us."

He wanted to say something, a little crease between his eyebrows. People communicate so much with their eyes, and their eyebrows, more than they do by talking.

"I think Connie's crazy not to live with you," I said.

His expression lightened. "You'd like her. Maybe I'll have her over tomorrow . . ."

"That's a good idea," I said, and he knew me well enough to shut up. He could tell. Maybe he wasn't conscious of it, but he could tell what was going to happen. He stood there for a while, feeling this doubt, this awareness.

And then he went into his room, turning the lights off as he went.

I slept.

It was automatic, even on the three bulging cushions, my body rising and falling unnaturally, a giant lying down on a countryside to sleep, having to put up with valleys and mesas, knee in the parking lot, ear in someone's front yard.

I woke and I could tell Ted wasn't asleep yet. I don't know how—I sensed it.

Maybe I was attuned to the rhythm of his breathing, used to it from the time I was an infant. We had to take naps, and I would lie beside my mother and hear her drift off, beginning to dream, my brother older, restless, playing with his cars and trucks in his bedroom until at last he was asleep, too, and the house belonged to me as I lay wide awake, the only one who was aware of the earth.

I was on my feet in the darkness, dressing quietly.

Lincoln was the hard part. As soon as I got up in the dark, he was jumping, frantic. Finally I seized his scruff, took a fistful of fur. I put my face down to his and hissed, "Sit still!"

He calmed down but continued to shiver with anticipation as I slipped on my shoes. There was a weak place in the floor, a soft place in the floorboards that sagged a little and creaked. I avoided it, and I avoided the angle of the coffee table in the darkness, quiet, like someone who wasn't really there.

Lincoln is too much trouble, I thought. Leave him here.

But he would yammer. The noisy, speechless animal would yowl, waking Ted. I gave him a pat, liking the way he leaned into me, still shivering a little, but trying to be patient.

I told him to stay where he was until I got back.

I could feel his doubt, his eagerness.

I told him again, in a low voice, like I would kill him if he moved.

It didn't take long. I knew what to do. When I had everything I needed, I walked as quietly as possible to the front door and turned the doorknob. I caught my breath, releasing the lock. It made a high-pitched squeak.

Lincoln was patient now, clued in on the general plan. His tail thumped the rug quietly. The lock was stuck. It was half steel, half rust, and no one had oiled it in decades. The walls of the house crept in a little closer, a worn-out bungalow with a landlord who lazed around in the desert and never dropped by to fix anything as obvious as a frozen deadbolt.

It squeaked again, but more faintly. There was a long moment of tension, Lincoln's tail thudding the floor.

And then I was outside.

The night was quiet, one cricket out by the curb. There was a whispery hush, a town asleep, a light on in a house at the end of the street.

I felt free, but I felt exposed, too. This time I wasn't just playing a private game with myself, a little test to see if I could make life a little more interesting, give the security people something to do.

Lincoln stayed right beside me, pressing against me as I yanked on the car door, having trouble getting it open. The car was parked at the curb, not parked all that well, the rear out too far. The car door was not locked. I might as well have put a sign on the windshield, HELP YOURSELF—FREE CAR.

The coyotes had stopped. The stars were shivering, the light still finding its way through the air pollution. The mountains were invisible, but it was easy to see where they were, blocking the stars.

Lincoln leaped into the car and took his seat on the passenger's side. I put the key in the ignition, and the Mustang whined, probably a remanufactured starter. I winced as the engine caught.

I knew it had awakened Ted. I knew my brother, and I knew he had been sleeping with a clear memory of how a Mustang would sound if it started up outside.

I made a quick inventory, map on the backseat, unfolded, spread all over the place, a little flattened. We had left Lincoln's rope—too bad, but maybe we wouldn't need it. Between Lincoln's legs was my straw purse with everything that would take me where I was going.

A light switched on in the house. I shifted the transmission out of park and into drive, and let the car roll away from the curb. I might have heard Ted calling me as I hit the accelerator harder than I wanted to, the car jerking out beyond the double line down the middle of the street.

I remembered to turn on the headlights after driving a few blocks, and I regretted having to do it. I asked myself if Ted would call the Highway Patrol to tell them his sister was on her way God knows where.

I wondered what they would tell him—that lost seventeen-year-old sisters were not a major problem, the world the way it is? I was pretty sure he'd call Dad, although maybe he'd wait until morning, let Dad have a night's sleep.

Maybe Mother had warned him that I was going to be more trouble than he imagined.

I pulled to the curb for half a minute. The interior light didn't work and probably hadn't worked for twenty years, the kind of thing nobody bothered to fix. A streetlight beside an elementary school shed just enough light to let me make sense out of the map. I tossed the map into the backseat, where it was a shape like a paper pyramid.

I made it to an on-ramp, the freeway familiar, a kind of homey feeling to the green, white-lettered signs. Some people spend years like this, driving from one place to another.

———

The traffic was not heavy, but it was still a surprise to see how many people were going someplace. It was easy for me to find the highway I wanted, following Interstate 15 toward Barstow. There was a mountain pass, vague shapes of hills beside the highway. If a Highway Patrol car was going to slip up from behind, it would be right about now.

Enough time had gone by for Ted to make his discovery, but I don't think he would really know what had happened until morning. Days might go by, because for all his intelligence and his ability to work hard, Ted believes in reality, that it basically makes sense. All you need is to get up in the morning and work, drag rocks, eat lunch in the sun.

It's a sure thing, Ted thinks: You save up money and after a while you go out and buy a nice new stereo television, and maybe a sofa you can lie down on without permanent paralysis.

Ted doesn't realize that Socrates's questionnaire, *How to Examine Your Life in Twenty Easy Steps,* was obsolete. It was missing a few pages that should have been collated over the centuries between then and now. The old philosopher had been teaching too long, handing out the same midterms to too many students.

I knew how it was done. I knew how to disappear.

I worked my hand into the purse and wrapped my fingers around the wad, the money I had stolen from Ted.

··· 29 ···

Every car looks like a police car from a distance.

They rise up out of nowhere, coast along in the rearview mirror. The old rearview didn't have an antiglare feature. You couldn't tilt it down and set it so headlights didn't blind. Cars crept up behind me, all light and mystery, and then they passed.

I kept steady, fifty-eight, fifty-nine miles per hour. I couldn't believe how hot it was. Night, day, it didn't matter to the desert.

Lincoln sat there stunned, his tongue hanging out. He pressed his nose against the window, smearing it with fresh snout prints. He smelled very much like a dog, and I wondered if they sold mouthwash for animals.

I was sticky, armpits, the insides of my thighs. My tongue was paste. I left the freeway in Barstow, found a Chevron station. I let Lincoln have a nice long drink from the rubber hose, and when the water splashed on me it felt good.

I pumped some super unleaded. I was going to check the fluid levels, the coolant, the oil, but a police car cruised by, looking at people on the sidewalk, slowing to look at the gas station, checking out every living thing, so I made it quick. I hurried to the pay booth and peeled off some money.

There was a lot of it. Ted had saved for a long time.

I could hear my dad's voice: Watch the fluid levels. If the car gets overheated, you're in trouble.

I could hear Ted's voice going on about how good Mahler would sound when he had new speakers, a better television.

The woman in the booth said something to me, talking into a microphone, her voice coming out of a speaker. I didn't understand what she was saying, this loud, brassy voice from someone right in front of me like bad lip-synching.

"Have a good evening," she was saying, a woman with drawn-on eyebrows, her natural brows growing in, needing to be shaved.

She was a little heavy, pretty in a tired way, up all night selling gas. People lived like this, I thought. They start out fresh and full of excitement and pretty soon they're repeating themselves into microphones in the heat, trying to be polite.

One of the chilling things about having a brother is that you know how he thinks. You know he keeps his savings in the closet. And you know it won't be long before he makes the discovery. He'll pace for a while, swearing in a fierce whisper the way Dad does when he's mad.

He'll be in among the pile of shoes, tossing aside those worn work boots, fumbling into his black oxfords, the ones like new because he never puts them on.

What will he do then? I asked myself.

What would I do?

I would call the police, everyone. I would never forgive.

I didn't want to think this way, but I even found myself standing in front of a telephone. I associate night with cool weather, but this was like inhaling for the first time, hot cigarette smoke all the way into the lungs. I stared at the phone, running my mother's phone number through my head, telling myself I couldn't remember it, but I could.

In my mind I heard the phone ringing. I saw Adler stirring, thinking it must be a patient of his, an emergency, expecting an answering service, answering the phone half-awake and concerned.

I could talk to him, that's what I would do. I could tell him how I felt. I could explain, and Adler would be understanding. He knew things. He might have guessed how I felt by now. That was it: He already knew. It would be a relief to have it all out in the open.

In my mind I had Adler and my mother married for years, a dresser packed with his shirts and her sweaters, folded neatly, fresh from the cleaners, the dresser top crowded with framed pictures, both of them smiling.

The handle of the car was warm, almost hot. Nobody could stand to live here, and yet there were people out on the sidewalks, one of them sitting on the curb, drinking from a can in his hand. Up the street the police had found what they wanted, talking to a group of men.

I drove slowly. One of the policemen let a flashlight beam shine upward, into a man's face. The man's features were illuminated, shadows cast upward so his face was a mask. He was explaining something to the police with no apparent concern, talking his way out of it.

The police were busy. But not so busy that one of them didn't look my way as I waited for the light to change from red to green.

Even the sound of the engine attracted attention sometimes, a solid rumble the newish muffler didn't do much to disguise. The cop took a long look, liking what he saw, maybe, enjoying the sight of a woman in a classic Mustang, and maybe starting to wonder. I felt tight inside.

The light was green. I let myself go slow, forced myself to drive by the book, letting the signal blink for a while before I changed lanes, left the city street, took the on-ramp toward Bishop and Las Vegas.

It didn't take long.

The car was handling funny, the engine surging. I recalled Mr. Friedlander's lecture on overheating, how the engine gets hot in traffic, and in hot weather waiting for lights to change, so I told myself that this was happening now.

All the engine needed was a little highway speed, let the radiator do its work. As a student, I was the one who could flush a cooling system. The temperature gauge was permanently stuck right in the middle, never showing hot or cold, one of about a thousand things wrong with this car.

I took an off-ramp and pulled over for a while at the edge of the desert. Lincoln put his snout in my face, worried I was going to get out, worried I was going to leave him.

"Just letting the car cool," I said.

I didn't get out of the car. I just sat there, and every now and then a long diesel truck would roar by on the freeway, pinpricks of red on the corners of the trailer.

What a mistake it is to sit here, I told myself. What did I think they would do when they caught me, give me a prize, the best daughter, the greatest sister, in North America?

I heard the Mom-voice start up in me. *If they want you they'll find you.* I didn't start driving again even though I thought the car was cool now and it was safe.

Coolant. I should have put in more coolant, but that didn't matter. The road behind me was closing in, my brother on the phone to the police, the police already on the road.

I got into the car and accelerated hard just as my mother's voice told me I didn't know what I was doing.

As the needle climbed past sixty, the car drifted, all the way over to the fast lane.

··· 30 ···

The police would not turn on their flashing lights until they got close. They would use stealth, lull me into thinking there was no danger. It was like being in a department store again, the jewelry department, knowing that the security people are closing in.

Lincoln knew before I was really aware of it—I was going too fast.

It didn't bother me. Speed was a kind of control. I kept the car straight down the fast lane, the headlights catching the reflection of litter in the center of the freeway, broken glass, scraps of chrome streaking by, a blur.

The Porta-Mom was full speed now. *Go ahead, if you're so sure of yourself. Go ahead and see what happens.*

The steering wheel vibrated, but I gripped it hard. Maybe Ted would tell them I was dangerous, I thought. He would have them arrest me because he thought I was going to hurt myself. He didn't know me very well after all, I thought, wishing I could say something to him, something to calm him down, shut him up.

Lincoln put his snout into my ear and made a huffy bark, not wanting to deafen me with a full-throated version. Then he whined. He looked this way and that, worked his way into the backseat, the map crinkling under his weight.

The radio was completely dead. I couldn't get a sound out of it. At about ninety, the car stopped going any faster, began to lose power a little, and then the engine recovered, the speedometer needle falling easily toward one hundred. With the car going this fast, the vibration evened out, the ride a lot more smooth. I made the little adjustments in steering, a little to the left, a little to the right.

"What's the matter?" I asked Lincoln, knowing I could reassure him. I reached back to him with one hand. He was frantically shifting his weight from side to side. The map tore, and tore again, as he tossed around in the backseat. He gave my fingers a lick, but he wouldn't sit still.

I sighed. I would be patient with my animal companion, show him what a sweet-tempered mistress I could be. I was already being patient with the way he smelled, not exactly like the perfume department.

Lincoln uttered one of his dog words, a moaning, howling bark that sounded almost comical, the world-famous Talking Dog.

"Hungry?"

I didn't like the thought of that. There was nothing to eat. Maybe he had to pee.

I took a firm grip on the wheel as I scented something.

It was like knowing the store has its cameras on me, knowing they see what my hands are doing even when I don't. I let the car gain speed even as I stopped thinking about what I was doing, watching the rearview every few seconds to see another car that looked like a police car fade away, unable to close in.

But now I smelled fire.

Litter from the center divide made a hiss under the wheels. It was time to slow down. It was time to ease back over to the slow lane, take another off-ramp, let the car cool.

That's what I wanted to do. But that's not what happened.

··· 31 ···

There was something in the road, a black half circle, all that was left of a tire. I didn't even see it until I was past it. I swerved, the car slipped sideways, the wheels screaming. I knew I would slow down now. Just a little slower, maybe let the needle slip back down toward eighty, maybe seventy.

I tried to reassure myself that I was slowing down. My foot was lifting off the pedal, and I could relax. But my foot stayed right where it was. I watched myself driving, and then my hands were alive, and I wasn't.

I watched what they did, how they turned the wheel hard. I watched what happened next, how they had felt this coming, planned it, the lanes of the freeway vanishing.

The car spun, the tires singing. The car swung all the way around. Headlights coming toward me, glittering. Then the car swung all the way back, full circle, the lanes of the freeway streaking under me.

Control. I had to get control of the car. And I remembered Mr. Friedlander's lecture, *turning into a skid stops it* When the car started to swing around again, I made myself steer in the direction of the skid.

The car stopped in its slow rotation and slid sideways until I wrestled the wheel again. There was a stink of tire rubber as I fought the car over to the edge of the road, still going too fast.

Feather the brakes, I reminded myself.

Way too fast.

The car flattened something, a sign. You're doing fine, I could hear my father say. Easy. Little by little. An orange plastic bag full of litter was ahead of me and then I could feel it explode under the car. Trash fluttered in the red glow of the brake light in the rearview.

I feathered the brakes again. The highway was off to the left, receding. Brush slapped the bottom of the car. A chain-link fence veered toward me, brilliant in the headlights, and veered away. The ride was rough, the wheel jerking out of my grip.

The chain-link fence swerved in, and this time I hit the brakes hard. My face struck the steering wheel, everything in the car flung forward. Lincoln slammed against the dash.

Even then we didn't stop, a smell of dust, the car plowing forward with locked wheels.

We stopped. The car was filled with a booming voice, a yelling, demented god. It was a shock, and for a moment I couldn't identify where the voice was coming from. I twisted knobs until the radio was off.

The engine was rattling, and there was a fluttery whisper from somewhere under the hood. I set the parking brake out of habit, and turned off the headlights. I switched off the engine. The silence was solid.

Lincoln was in the backseat again, snout in my ear. He was shuddering. I let myself droop against the steering wheel. Lincoln was making a high, reedy whistle through his nostrils. "It's all right," I told him.

The dog argued, whining, yammering, then gave up being polite and barked.

He was so loud my ears rang. I told him to shut up

and I seized the door handle and gave it a good tug. The door wouldn't open.

I told myself to wait a second, get a better grip, try it again. The air tasted bitter. I knew the car was going to burn.

···32···

The engine was making sounds like a long breath being let out and then being let out some more. There was a smell in the air, hot metal, chemical steam. The gearshift between the seats dug into my back. All these months, I told myself, I should have been jogging, getting ready for this.

My feet hurt, and the side window waggled back and forth each time I kicked it, but nothing else happened. At last it started to crack, and finally one last kick and there were glass pebbles all over the front seat, all over me. I pulled at chunks of the glass, the stuff bending back and forth, fighting back. It broke away in my hands.

I knew what would happen next. A burning car hisses and squeals, rubber and plastic and grease sizzling. After it burns for a while it blows up.

I fell, hard. I was dizzy. It was cool out here, the gravel at my cheek. I coughed, inhaling sand. Lincoln tumbled out of the car after me.

This was when it would explode.

I got up and ran. I didn't run very well, some of the dead plants stretching long, skinny branches that caught at me. We were farther from the highway than I had expected, scruffy weeds and sand underfoot. The earth was uneven, with bare places with nothing but gravel, and what looked like old beer cans in the starlight.

Blood was running from my nose. I slowed to a walk, crunching dead weeds and baked plastic bags underfoot. I brushed fragments of glass off my front. When I reached the edge of the freeway I was sure someone would stop, but a car passed and didn't even slow.

Lincoln stayed close, and when I looked down at him he looked up at me, *Now what*?

There were so many stars. I tilted my head to look and stayed like that for a while. A truck rumbled by on the freeway, and I was sure it would stop, sure that everyone could see the Mustang stuck in the middle of the desert, but nobody saw. It was the same color as much of the sand, dead white. It was like being nowhere.

The blood from my nose was beginning to dry, the clotting factors you read about in detective stories, the blood proteins going to work. It gave me a good idea how much time was passing. The edge of the freeway was strewn with bits of glass among the coiled fan belts and ribbons of tire rubber. A bone stuck out of what looked like a scrap of fur.

I kept looking back at the car, expecting fire, but nothing happened. The sight of the car hooked me, hurting. It was the car my father had given me, my father planning the purchase, keeping it secret, leading me out onto the front lawn that Sunday afternoon. I remembered his smile, his shy, "What do you think?"

Minutes were passing and no one stopped. I hadn't pictured desert like this, Barstow a scuzzy glow of lights to the west. There was a flattened cardboard box so old and dried out it was stuck to the sand. There wasn't even that much traffic now, and when a truck approached I could hear it long before I could see it, an engine getting closer and closer and then sweeping by me with a sudden, dry wind, grit in the air.

When someone spoke to me, I didn't bother to answer at first. I had turned into someone who was doing nothing but waiting, standing, not expecting anything.

Maybe it hadn't even been that long, ten minutes, twenty. I had the vague impression of a recreational vehicle, one of those metal houses on wheels, parked way up on the road. The voice belonged to a woman, and I turned to look at her when I realized that she was close to me, saying something in a soft voice.

"That your car?" she said, just confirming something. She was just a person, not a cop, T-shirt, short pants, rubber thongs on her feet.

I could speak. "It's mine," I said.

"Was there anyone else inside?" Gravel was creeping between her rubber soles and her feet, and she stood on one leg, took off her rubber sandal and shook out a pebble.

There was Lincoln, I wanted to say, but he was sitting there, made nervous by the woman, peering at her from behind me.

"Just you and the dog," the woman said, answering for me.

The way I nodded made her put out a hand, touching me lightly on the arm. "Are you all right?"

··· 33 ···

I was waiting for Ted.

It was cool where I was, even a little cold, the air conditioner doing too good a job. Sometimes a car would pass on the road beyond the parking lot, a small pickup, and I was sure this was Ted. But for a long time it wasn't, and people came into the room, people in uniform eating Chee-tos, while I breathed against the glass. I watched cars go back and forth in the smog.

And then he was there. Ted got out of his pickup and tucked in his shirt where it had slipped out. He ran his hand over his hair. He took off his dark glasses and folded them, and put them carefully in his shirt pocket. He squinted now in the morning sunlight, walking briskly through the heat.

I could see him through the tinted glass from the snack room, a long cafeteria table and vending machines, Fritos, Coke. There was a sign on the wall, SAFETY BELTS ARE LAW. I didn't want him to know I had been standing there, waiting. I unfolded a newspaper, want ads, crossword puzzles. My purse was on the corner of the table.

I noticed the shoes when he came into the room. I also noticed how much he looked like Mother, not just like Dad. He had the same way of smiling when he wasn't happy.

He was wearing his dress shoes, the black oxfords.

"You got dressed up," I said. "Nice slacks."

Ted smiled, but his eyes were bloodshot.

"I look terrible," I said, before he could say anything else.

"You look wonderful to me," he said.

I folded up the newspaper carefully, a neat pile, the tiny printing of the want ads, the crossword puzzle with its blank spaces. "They said they'd x-ray my nose if I wanted, but they were sure it isn't broken."

"I have some stain remover at home," he said.

I glanced down at my dress. It was going to take a professional cleaner to rescue this silk. It was probably hopeless. "They towed the car." I was going to add that it was at a Chevron station with a snapped axle and an engine that would have to be replaced.

"We can talk about it later," he said. It was nice to sound like this, two smart people playing Conversation, *"fun for the entire family."*

Something about him irritated me. Maybe he thought it was no use telling me what he thought. Maybe he thought I was emotionally disturbed and a frank talk would be too much for me to take. Maybe the Highway Patrol officers had said as much: You've got a really shaken young woman there, Mr. Charles.

"I think you'll feel better after a shower," he said. "Use some of that soap Connie left."

I held on to the table. It was one of those indestructible surfaces, false wood grain, a shiny metal strip all the way around the edge. Someone had spilled some coffee days ago, and it was still there, a beige scab.

Ted sat down next to me, patient. But not really patient, I thought, acting patient, because he thought that was what I needed. Maybe he just wanted to get out of here.

Ted didn't say anything, just looked at me and took my hand. It was this gesture that made me look away and close my eyes. He held one of *those*, one of the hands that lied to me.

It's amazing how my voice can sound sometimes, calm, smooth, and other times I can hardly get a word out. This time I sounded okay—not great, but pretty good. "Your money's in my purse," I said.

He nodded wearily. It took what seemed like an hour, but at last he said, "The money doesn't matter."

"Of course it matters," I said. "What if I said I threw

it all away, flung it into the wind as I drove along the freeway? What if I said the car burned up, and all the money?"

"I'd say we should look in your purse, see if it's there."

I gave him a look: Okay, maybe you're right.

"Where's the dog?" he asked.

"He couldn't stay in the food service area," I said, "because of the health laws."

"So what did they do, shoot him?"

It was a terrible thing to say, but I couldn't help laughing, just sitting there for a moment with my brother.

It was hot out. Lincoln was in the shade behind a building, tied up with bright nylon rope. Someone had given him a big clean ashtray full of water, and a box of dried cat food. There was nothing left of the cat food but chewed-up cardboard.

I waited for Ted to unlock the pickup. The top of the Highway Patrol building was a collection of antennas and satellite dishes. It was amazing that so many words could be coursing through the sunlight, but I couldn't feel any of them.

Ted said, "We'll pick up Dad at the airport about noon."

We picked up Dad, the airport parking lot crowded, Dad standing outside Arriving Flights with one of his expressions, his face calm so you don't know what he's thinking.

There was so much smog we couldn't see the mountains in the distance. We were all three in the cab of the truck, and that kept us quiet, talking about safe subjects, traffic, sports—magic talk—making troubles go away for a few minutes.

As we swung into Ted's neighborhood, Dad said, "The insurance company will take care of everything."

I almost felt sorry for him. He thought maybe that was all he had to say, explain how a procedure would take care of everything, the legal mind. *Everything'll be okay—all we have to do is fill out this form.* I tried to picture myself six months, a year from then, and my mind was a blank.

In the shower you can forget there is a life out there, streets and houses. There is nothing but the hot water, and the steamy air.

I took a long time drying myself, and I could hear them. They were talking, the two of them—contractors' licenses, night classes in accounting. I wiped the mirror and looked at myself.

I made my entrance, drying my hair. Dad was sitting on the couch, his hands in his lap. He was looking at me, his gaze steady. He met my eyes and did not look away. The three of us made the living room seem crowded.

I sat there in one of Ted's V-neck T-shirts and a pair of his jeans, the legs rolled up. When I moved a leg the denim hung baggy and loose, like I had lost thirty pounds overnight.

I got up and went outside, Lincoln slobbering on my fingers. Dad followed me, as I had wanted him to, and I stood outside on the concrete slab. The hibiscus had lost all of its blossoms, little yellow scraps on the concrete, fragments of popped balloons.

It's the kind of neighborhood that isn't very peaceful, babies crying, distant laughter, a helicopter clopping along over the freeway far away. A swing set creaked, and somewhere children were having fun, splashing in a backyard pool or running through a sprinkler.

I could hear Dad right behind me, his shadow beside mine. "I'm in love with Adler," I said.

Okay, I had said it. I could go back in the house now, I thought. The main thing was to keep moving.

But I wasn't shutting up. I was talking. I told him everything, worked quickly, nailing in all the facts, how I couldn't possibly live with Mom and Adler, feeling the way I did. I didn't tell them about my hands, how they lied to me, how they almost got me killed. I couldn't talk about that.

I didn't look at him when I was talking, so when he put his hands on my shoulders and turned me around I was a little surprised. He put his arms around me. He didn't even say anything for a long time, just held me there, his cheek against my wet hair, swaying a little like someone who didn't know how to slow-dance.

After a long time, he said, "Stay with me."

I thought I had misunderstood him. He sounded so different.

My voice sounded weak. "Mom won't understand."

He made a gesture with his hand, *maybe, maybe not.* "She will," he said. "Anna—what matters is you."

I shook my head and looked away. It wasn't that simple.

I wanted to tell him it wouldn't work, that he was wrong, that I was more troubled than he knew.

I looked at him, and I could tell what he was thinking—that he wanted me to be safe, he wanted me to have a future, and so I cried.

Then, when I could, I smiled and lied a little, and told him maybe things would work out, pretending I believed it.

··· 35 ···

The most interesting moment of all is when I walk into a store and the security stiffens. One moment it's a placid department store, wristwatches 30 percent off, and the next you can hear them think: She's here.

I was nervous, but not about the house detectives.

In the six months since my return, I had kept away from places like this. I had nearly forgotten what it was like, the tables of sportswear, the mannequins. I stood by a table of cashmere-and-kidskin gloves, *reduced to clear*, waiting for the Capwell's Emporium floorwalkers to close in. Security people had spotted me. They weren't very good at it, overreacting, watching me too carefully.

I made it to the escalator and rode it to the second floor, enjoying that emotional lift I always get from automatic stairs, getting somewhere without moving.

I thought, how thrilling. Now I can steal a pillow or a huge, ugly lamp.

Kitchen tables. Microwaves. Gleaming Farberware pots, enough to hold eight cabbages, eight human heads, all that capacity, and with a nonstick surface.

I couldn't believe Maureen was bargain hunting. Maybe it was amusing for her: *Why spend more for a butcher-block table than we have to. They have one on sale in El Cerrito.*

But I knew the real reason for our shopping trip. Maureen and I had slowly rebuilt our friendship, but Mr. Dean had avoided me, not speaking to me as he passed me on his bike.

I must have said something about this to Maureen. "Meet me there," she had said. "I'll bring him along."

And maybe Maureen was challenging me a little, letting me find out what it would be like to be in a kingdom of merchandise again.

The man in the camel's-hair jacket had restless eyes. He had that look of the teacher monitoring the IQ tests, watching for people to whisper the answer, *egg is to bird as fire is to what.*

The clerk in Kitchens for Today didn't know the rules. She was my age, maybe a little older. Her Capwell's Emporium name tag said her name was Denise. Not only new, but there was a little word under her name. Trainee.

I asked, "Are these the ones on sale?"

"I think they might be. . . ."

She wasn't just a trainee clerk. She was a trainee human being, her first day.

"Fifty percent off," I read from a sign in red-and-black letters. "Do they come assembled?"

"They come knocked down," said Denise, reading from the same sign.

"In a box, instructions, one-two-three," I said.

Denise gave a little laugh. She had heard all about customers. They say stupid things, and all the retail pro can do is show good manners.

I ran one finger along the cute little Krups coffee grinder, its white cord plugged into an electric outlet in the floor. The camel's-hair man was on the other side of the display. "Is there anything special we can do for you today?"

"Don't you have any larger butcher-block tables?" I said. "I like the little wheels. I can wheel my chopped meat from the laundry room to the garage; I can see the convenience. But the ad in the paper made the table look so much more substantial."

"Let me give you one of our catalogs on the way out," he said.

Security men so often have no names, just jackets, faces. They ship people like this in cartons, snap them together and watch the shoplifters flee.

"I think we have a case of false advertising," I said.

Joe Camel didn't even try to smile. "We'll ask the manager," he said.

"The ad right here taped to this table said it's eighteen inches across," I said.

"Why don't we step this way," said a man behind me, a stealth walker. He came from the mattress section, surprising me. He was one I recognized from my old days here. "See if the manager can answer your questions."

"This is the table?" said a voice.

The two men turned and adopted casual postures, adjusting a tie, fiddling with a sleeve.

Maureen was dressed in a camouflage outfit, desert camouflage, ready for dune warfare. I had never seen her quite like this. She was wearing purple-and-black basketball shoes.

Her father was with her, wearing his gray suit, but without his tie today.

Mr. Dean did not smile. "Hello, Anna," he said.

I said something, *hello*, or I asked how he was. I heard myself uttering some sort of response. All I could think was: I'm talking to both of them at last.

"Maureen was telling me you think—heh—I've been avoiding you." His little laugh came out joyless.

"I wouldn't blame you," I said.

I could see conflict of feelings in his eyes. He might never forgive me for taking Lincoln, but he could not bear to be totally impolite, even to someone he didn't like.

"I've always envied your family," I said. "For being so happy."

I offered my hand, and he took it. We shook hands before the two security men like two diplomats.

"I don't think that table's big enough," said Mr. Dean.

He was pretending he was forgiving me, and it worked. His eyes were warmer now, sincere. Sometimes it starts that way, you just decide to go along and see what happens.

"What do you think?" said Maureen, looking at the table as though she could destroy it with one blow.

"I think your father deserves something better than a little table like this," I said.

···36···

"You ought to do a show about where men buy those one-size-too-big camel's-hair jackets," I said. "Show all the bald camels in the desert, shivering."

Mother and I were having lunch on Solano Avenue. It was the day after my shopping trip with Maureen and her father.

Mother and I were both eating salad, lettuce and bean sprouts all over the place. This was a new place, where Maxi's used to be. It had silver salt and pepper shakers, tall and tapered, heavy in the hand. There was a silver holder for the packets of sugar. It was not sterling, but it was good.

"How is Adler?" I asked.

"His indigestion acts up all the time," she said. "He eats antacids like candy. Otherwise . . ."

It was time for a napkin to my lips, a sip of ice water. I didn't think about Adler as often, but his name still set off currents in me, tides of color, like the surface of Jupiter.

It looked like two heads of lettuce had exploded. The bowls were small and the salad was huge. A ring of red onion slid from my salad onto the white table-cloth.

"You and Maureen get along these days," she said. It was a suggestion, not a question. I wondered if she was relieved that I wasn't moving in with her.

This was one of my easy moments, enjoying Mom's company. That was when I started to worry most, when my emotional weather was sunny.

As we were ready to leave, I found myself carrying the silverware to the plastic tub. The guy in the white apron busing dishes smiled, a tall guy, black hair. He was folding a new white tablecloth over a table. He thought I was being helpful.

I checked when I was out on the sidewalk.

"Did you forget something?" Mother asked, putting on her sunglasses, ready to go back to Channel Two and have them tear up a parking lot.

It was windy outside, bright sun and chilly air. We

stood at the corner of Solano and Colusa. I fumbled through my purse. There was a new wallet, gleaming house key, no car keys to worry about anymore. Compact, brush, Dentyne, matches I picked up somewhere thinking I still smoked.

"Anna, are you all right?" Mom asked.

It wasn't a simple question, and she knew it. "How many people do you think walk off with one of their forks?" I said. "Or one of those salt and pepper shakers?"

My mother looked strained and slipped off her sunglasses to study me. "I couldn't begin to guess," she said.

I turned to tell her not to worry, but the sun was so bright I had to close my eyes for a second, thinking what an idiot I was to forget my glasses. Maybe I would buy a pair of sunglasses, cheap ones, just for today. The sound of the traffic was loud, something you realized only when you stopped looking. And there was the tree in Andronico's across the street, the redwood full of birds. Even without looking I could tell so much about the street, the traffic, someone laughing, all of it okay. Or maybe not okay, something terrible about to happen.

When I opened my eyes I stopped really listening, waiting for the traffic light to change.